"*Emma . . .*" *Kurt began.*

He stared at her. Then before she knew what was happening, he got down on one knee.

"*What are you doing?*" *she asked him.*

"*Emma . . .*" *Kurt began again, gazing up at her.*

She shivered a little in her T-shirt and rubbed at her arms. "*Yes, Sir Galahad.*" *She giggled.* "*Am I supposed to knight you?*"

But Kurt's face was very serious. "*Emma Cresswell, I love you very much, and I will honor you forever,*" *he said.*

Emma's heart began thudding in her chest. Her eyes grew huge and her hands began to shake as realization dawned on her. Oh, my God, she thought. Oh, my God, he's going to . . .

Kurt took her hand and kissed it. "*Emma, my love, will you marry me?*"

Sunset Wedding

CHERIE BENNETT

Sunset™ Island

SPLASH™

B

A BERKLEY / SPLASH BOOK

SUNSET WEDDING is an original publication of
The Berkley Publishing Group.
This work has never appeared before in book form.

SUNSET WEDDING

A Berkley Book / published by arrangement with
General Licensing Company, Inc.

PRINTING HISTORY
Berkley edition / November 1993

A GLC BOOK

Splash and *Sunset Island* are
trademarks belonging to
General Licensing Company, Inc.

ISBN: 0-425-13982-4

BERKLEY®
Berkley Books are published
by The Berkley Publishing Group,
200 Madison Avenue, New York, New York 10016.
BERKLEY and the "B" design
are trademarks belonging to Berkley Publishing Corporation.

PRINTED IN THE UNITED STATES OF AMERICA

10 9 8 7 6 5 4 3 2 1

Special thanks to the Peace Corps
for providing me with
application information

This book is for my partner in crime

Sunset Wedding

ONE

"You should be a stripper," Carrie Alden decisively told her best friend Emma Cresswell over the phone.

"I should do *what*?" Emma asked.

"Become a stripper," Carrie repeated playfully. "You said to help you think up some great career goals, and I'm helping."

"Gee, that's one profession that never occurred to me," Emma said dryly.

"I can see it now on a Las Vegas marquee: 'Tonight, live on stage: See Emma Cresswell, Boston Ice Princess! See *all* of Emma Cresswell, Boston Ice Princess.'"

"You know, you're starting to sound distinctly like Sam," Emma told Carrie, referring to their wild and audacious friend, Samantha Bridges.

"Yeah, you're right," Carrie said with a laugh. "But maybe that means she'll start sounding like me, and she'll go back to college!"

Emma switched the phone from her left ear

1

to her right. "Speaking of college," Emma said with a sigh, "I'm sitting here staring at my Goucher College catalogue for the fall and it's truly depressing!" Emma flipped through the pages of the catalogue half-heartedly.

"In that case, don't rule out stripping," Carrie said with mock solemnity. "Why go back to college and be depressed? And just think of all the money you'd make!"

"I don't need money," Emma answered. "I have to keep reminding my mother not to send any to me."

"A pleasant problem," Carrie said. "Look, you mean there's nothing in the catalogue you want to take next year?"

Emma stared down at the catalogue. She'd opened to Modern European History. "Well, if there is I haven't found it yet," Emma replied.

She heaved a sigh and flipped to another page in the catalogue. *This is turning into a pity party for one,* she thought to herself. *I should be glad that my college catalogue arrived so I can preregister. I should be glad that I don't have to worry about how I'm going to pay for school. I should realize how lucky I am!*

"You still there?" Carrie called into the phone.

"Yes," Emma replied, "and listen, I'm sorry to be whining so much—"

"Hey, you're entitled," Carrie said lightly. "You are a singularly non-whiney kind of person."

"It's just that you know I'd rather be going to Africa this fall than back to Goucher," Emma said earnestly.

"Look, Emma," Carrie said, "if that's what you—uh-oh." Emma heard the phone drop and the sound of a little girl crying.

"Sorry, Emma," Carrie's voice came through again. "I think Chloe just wiped out on the stairs. Call you later."

"Bye!" Emma said as Carrie hung up.

Emma walked over to the window in her room in the Hewitts' house, and looked out at the front yard.

What right do I have to be complaining? she asked herself again. *I can afford to go to school, I have two of the best friends in the world, an amazingly cool boyfriend, and the ultimate summer job.*

Sometimes Emma had a hard time believing how good her situation was—the fact that she still wasn't satisfied made her feel doubly irritated now.

She was back on glamorous Sunset Island, a fabulous resort island off the coast of southern Maine, for the second summer in a row. She was working as an au pair for a really great family, the Hewitts—Jane and Jeff Hewitt were lawyers in Portland when they weren't summering on the island, and they were the most unpretentious adults she'd ever met. They were smart, funny,

3

honest, and down to earth. Their three kids, Ethan, Wills, and Katie, were really sweet—well, most of the time, anyway. Of course, Emma's mother thought it was absurd that her daughter wanted to work—their family was one of the richest in America—but then, Kat Cresswell thought it was absurd that anyone would want to work. But Emma felt differently, and in taking the job, had finally done something that *she* wanted.

Emma's two best friends, Carrie Alden and Sam Bridges, were back on the island too. Emma thought it was amazing how the three of them were so different but still best friends— Sam with her outrageous personality and wild red hair, and dark-haired, girl-next-door Carrie, who was smart and talented and the most level-headed person Emma had ever met. *And then there's me*, Emma thought to herself. *Product of European boarding schools and every luxury in the world, blond-haired, well-groomed, and— everyone thinks—cool and controlled. Ha. I don't see myself that way at all. There are so many things I don't have a clue about. But one thing I do know—the greatest day of my life was the day I met Sam and Carrie at the International Au Pair Convention in New York. That's when everything began to change.*

Emma stare out at the perfect, sunny day. She thought about what her boyfriend, Kurt

Ackerman, was doing right at that moment. *Probably at the country club teaching some little girl to swim,* Emma thought with a smile. Kurt was so good with little girls.

He's also good with big girls, she thought wickedly, *like me, for instance.* She closed her eyes and remembered what it felt like when Kurt kissed her. It was delicious. *Kurt is so fabulous,* she thought dreamily. *Smart, kind, sensitive, and gorgeous—just about every girl on the island is after him. So, we've had a few fights. What couple hasn't? He's always been there for me.*

Emma sighed and opened her eyes. She looked back at the college catalogue on her bed and got depressed all over again.

She had been hoping to be able to study anthropology in France with Dr. Chanderot, who was the leader in the field. But as luck would have it, he was on sabbatical for the upcoming semester, so it looked like she was stuck at Goucher. Like a little child, she stuck her tongue out at the offending book. *Oh, very mature, Emma,* she chided herself. *Just sit down and shut up and pick out your fall classes.*

But she couldn't help it. The very thought of it made her feel sick to her stomach.

"Stop it! Just stop it!" she said out loud, as if she could talk herself into an attitude change. Resolutely she marched over to the bed, sat down, and

5

picked up the preregistration material.

It seemed to her like it was pretty early for catalogues to go out, but a letter that came with the materials said Goucher was trying out a new preregistration system, and all students had to fill out and return their forms early.

Emma picked up the first form. DECLARATION OF MAJOR, it said on it.

Uh-oh, she thought. *Problem number one. My mother wants me to be a French major. All the women in my family have been French majors. In fact, all the women in my family have been French majors at Goucher. And my mother is good friends with the president of the college. So if I declare any major other than French, she'll find out about it right away. And if I tell her that I'm skipping the next two years of school to go work in Africa for the Peace Corps . . .*

Just then the phone rang. Emma glanced at the clock: 5:15 P.M. The Hewitts were all spending the afternoon at a multiple-family picnic on the beach, but they were due back by 5:30.

If it's for me, I can't talk long, Emma thought.

"Hewitt residence, Emma Cresswell speaking," Emma answered, reaching for a pad and a pen in case there was any message.

"Take it off! Take it all off!" a familiar voice sang out on the phone. "Do it, baby, do it!"

"Hi, Sam," Emma said, her voice full of mock exasperation.

6

"Emma," Sam said, "I didn't realize that Goucher offered a major in exotic dancing. Does your mother know about this?"

"I take it you've been talking to Carrie," Emma replied.

"Right-amundo," Sam confirmed. "Listen, my advice is don't get all bent out of shape over this college stuff. I wouldn't."

"Of course you wouldn't," Emma said with a laugh. "You dropped out."

"Don't bother me with petty details," Sam said airily.

"I've got to figure out what I'm going to do," Emma said.

"Why?" Sam asked. "I never figure out what I'm going to do ahead of time. It ruins all spontaneity."

"I know, you're not a real plan-ahead kind of babe," Emma said, quoting an often-uttered Sam-ism.

"Right!" Sam agreed.

"I thought you were talking about going back to dancing at Disney World," Emma reminded her. Sam had worked as a show dancer at Disney World the previous year, but had what she'd termed a personality conflict with the chief choreographer. He fired her for being too original. Now, there was a new choreographer in charge, and Sam had talked about giving it another chance.

"Well, I don't know," Sam mused. "It would be pretty weird, after what happened with Danny, you know?"

Emma knew what Sam meant. Sam's friend from Disney World, Danny Franklin, had recently visited the island. Danny was crazed for Sam, and Sam really cared for him, but she had finally decided she liked him only as a friend. Danny had been crushed.

"You shouldn't let what happened with Danny stop you from doing what you want to do," Emma told Sam.

"Whatever," Sam replied. "I'm still hoping to hit the Tri-State lottery. Hey, maybe you can support me for a year or so."

"If I decide to major in zoology or anthropology instead of French and my mother finds out," Emma retorted, "you may need to support me."

"Hey, I know!" Sam cried. "We can become exotic dancers together!"

"I'll pass," Emma said.

"Got plans for later?" Sam asked.

"Not really, because—"

"Play Café, nine o'clock," Sam commanded, referring to the café that was their regular hang-out. "Be there or be square."

"But what if—"

"Gotta fly!" Sam said. "Bye!"

Emma shook her head at Sam's antics and hung up the phone.

She reached for the Declaration of Major form and smiled, suddenly remembering the anthropology teacher at her stuffy boarding school in Switzerland. Ms. Kramer, or Annabella, as she insisted her students call her, had been Emma's very favorite teacher. *Of course, all the teachers at Aubergame were excellent,* Emma reflected, *"the best money could buy,"* Daddy used to say. But it was Annabella Kramer who had given Emma her introduction to Dian Fossey's work with primates. And she was not just a good teacher, she was inspired.

Emma picked up a pen. Before she could stop herself, she wrote in big, block letters: PEACE CORPS.

Emma stared at what she had written. It felt right.

Guess I'll have some big news for Sam when I see her, Emma thought. *For a change, it's Emma Cresswell who's going to stir things up on this island. For once, I'm going to do exactly what I want!*

"I saw your stuff came from Goucher today," Jane Hewitt said to Emma, taking a bite of the pizza she had brought home as a light supper for the family.

"Is college fun?" seven-year-old Wills Hewitt asked Emma, reaching for another slice.

"It can be," Jeff Hewitt replied, seeing that Emma's mouth was full. "It can also be a big drag, if it's not where you want to be."

"I can't wait," Ethan Hewitt, age twelve, announced. "I'm going to Notre Dame and I'm gonna play football."

"Me, too," Wills said.

"Pick another school," Ethan ordered. "You can't go to my school."

"Football?" Jane asked. "Couldn't you think up some nice, non-dangerous activity to pursue?"

"Football scholarships, I like that idea," Jeff said.

"You would!" Jane laughed.

"Did you guys go straight through school?" Emma asked, taking a sip of iced tea.

"Yep," Jane replied. "Boston University."

"Nope," Jeff answered. "I went to VISTA."

"VISTA?" Emma asked.

"Volunteers In Service To America!" Jane sang out. "Like the Peace Corps, except it's in America."

"Dad was on an Indian reservation," Ethan explained, "teaching kids stuff."

"No kidding?" Emma marveled.

"I taught elementary ed," Jeff explained, cracking open a cold beer.

"Was it fun?" Emma asked.

"No," Jeff replied seriously, "but it's one of the greatest things I've ever done with my life."

"I don't think a lot of young people these days have much interest in VISTA," Jane said with shrug. "They all want to make a million bucks by the time they're thirty."

What if you already have a million bucks? Emma thought. *Or thirty million?*

"Well," Emma said hesitantly, "I'm thinking about the Peace Corps for next year. Instead of college."

"I don't know, Emma," Jeff said. "Doesn't the Peace Corps require a college degree, or some certain skill? Maybe you should wait until after you graduate."

"You didn't wait," Jane reminded her husband.

"That was different," Jeff retorted.

"No, it wasn't," Jane said matter-of-factly, putting some dessert tarts out on the table. "Anyway, isn't our friend John Harrison one of the chiefs of the Corps down in D.C.?"

"Yeah," Jeff recalled, "I think you're right."

Emma's heart leapt. If there were any rules that might otherwise bar her from the Peace Corps, maybe John Harrison would be able to help her.

"You really think you could call—" Emma began hesitantly.

Jane turned to her. "Of course we'll call for you."

"Just don't be disappointed if the college degree

thing turns out to be a hard and fast rule," Jeff warned.

"Do they play football in Africa?" Wills, who had been following the conversation with interest, asked. They all laughed.

"I really don't know," Emma said honestly.

"Hey, can we throw the ball around after dinner?" Ethan asked his dad. "You and me and not—" he shot Wills a dirty look "—you-know-who?"

"Yeah, we have to get you in shape for that scholarship!" Jeff teased.

"Me, too!" Wills chimed in. He reached for another strawberry tart. "After dessert."

"Let me and Carrie look into our crystal ball and tell you what is going to happen," Sam said to Emma over the din of the Play Café.

"First, you are going to tell your mother about the Peace Corps—" Carrie said, taking a bite of the nachos they'd ordered.

"And then, your mother is going to kill you," Sam finished. "You guys want to order some more nachos?"

"I hope the two of you don't charge for your fortune-telling," Emma said grimly. "I don't think you'd have a lot of customers."

"Oh, we only do this for close friends, right Sam?" Carrie asked.

"Right," Sam agreed. "And don't worry Emma,

we'll be right there with you to watch the carnage. After you're dead, we'll scatter your ashes, I promise."

"You're wonderful human beings," Emma said solemnly.

"We know," Sam said, craning her neck to look for the waitress. "Where's Patsi? I'm still hungry."

"You're always hungry," Carrie reminded her. "Don't let me eat anymore."

"Don't worry, I'll scarf them so fast you won't have a chance," Sam assured her; still looking for the waitress.

"You really think my mother is going to lose it?" Emma asked thoughtfully, sipping her iced tea.

"Well . . ." Carrie reflected slowly.

"I don't *think* that's what's going to happen," Sam said.

"Really?" Emma asked, hopefully.

"Really," Sam said. "I don't *think* that's what Kat will do. I *know* that's what Kat will do."

"Yeah," Emma ruminated, "you're probably right.

"The question is," Carrie said, sipping her diet Coke, "what is Kurt going to do? Have you told him yet?"

Emma shook her head.

No, I haven't told him, she thought. *The last time we had a serious talk about my joining, he looked like he was going to cry.*

"Knowing Kurt," Carrie stated, "I don't think he's going to be too happy."

"He'll have a cow," Sam said.

"I know!" Emma moaned, and buried her head in her arms. "Why does this have to be so hard?"

"Emma," Carrie asked, "how much do you want to go to Africa?"

Emma lifted her head. "More than anything else in the world," she answered fervently.

Sam took a bite of her garlic bread. "Then there's only one thing to do," she said.

"What's that?" Emma asked.

"Go, girlfriend, go!"

"Sam's right," Carrie said. "It's all you've ever talked about when you talk about the future. I don't think you have a choice."

"I can always go back to Goucher," Emma reasoned.

"And be miserable?" Sam reminded her.

"Yeah, that's right," Emma responded.

Sam took another bite of garlic bread. "Not that you'll be eating much garlic bread in Africa."

"I hear that there are some great bookstores in the Kenyan highlands," Carrie joked.

"Hold on, can you use a Visa card in Mozambique?" Sam queried. "Because that could be the deciding factor."

"Ugh," Carrie said. "I think Africa, I think bugs. Big, squishy, hairy, buzzing, bugs."

"You sure you really want to do this?" Sam asked Emma.

Emma got a really dreamy look on her face.

"Uh-oh," Carrie said, to no one in particular. "Look out—she's hooked. And Africa will never be the same."

"That's for sure," Emma responded. "Especially when I get Sam to come visit me there."

"The words Samantha Bridges and Africa have never been used in the same sentence before this moment," Sam commented. "As far as I'm concerned, that calls for another order of nachos."

"Do you have to?" Carrie groaned.

"Yes," Sam said emphatically. "We all have to. Soon we'll be visiting Emma in Africa, where I understand it is really difficult to get great nachos. Oh, waitress!"

TWO

"You're going to do *what*?" Kurt asked Emma, his voice full of incredulity.

"Take two years off from college and join the Peace Corps," Emma replied, trying to keep her voice even and her emotions under control.

Kurt took a glance around to make sure that none of the kids playing in the country club pool had gotten into trouble. Then he turned his attention back to Emma.

"Have you told your friends, or did you just save this bombshell for me?" he asked.

"It's not a bombshell," Emma said defensively. "We've talked about it a lot."

"Yeah, but you never presented it to me as some . . . forgone conclusion," Kurt snapped. He ran his fingers through his hair and noticed out of the corner of his eye a kid running near the side of the pool. "Hey, no running!" he yelled to the kid. He turned back to Emma. "Why the hell did you come here to tell me this?"

Emma fidgeted a bit as she stood near Kurt's

side. *Why did I want to tell him right away? Why did I pick this time and place?* she mused to herself. *What could have gotten into me?* She remembered waking up with a burning desire to talk to Kurt about her plans for the next school year, but now she regretted it.

"I'm sorry," Emma apologized. "I guess I should have waited until you weren't working."

Kurt folded his arms defensively. "So, did you already tell Sam and Carrie?"

"I told them last night, at the Play Café," Emma said honestly.

"Great, I'm the last one to know," Kurt replied sarcastically.

"That's not true!" Emma cried. "We've been talking about it all summer."

"I suppose that's true, though I never thought you'd decide to go in September. What's this going to mean for us?" Kurt asked, his voice growing quiet.

"We'll still be together," Emma assured him.

"Oh, Em, you know we've had this conversation before," Kurt said sadly. "Long-distance love doesn't work." Two kids were play-fighting each other near the shallow end of the pool. "Hey, Sarah!" he called to the other lifeguard on duty. "Can you watch the pool for a few minutes?"

"Sure," Sarah called back.

"I shouldn't have interrupted you at work—" Emma began.

"Well, too late now," Kurt replied tersely. "Where were we?"

"You were telling me that long-distance love doesn't work," Emma reminded him. "But . . . but last time we talked about this you said you'd try to understand—"

"And I have tried!" Kurt exclaimed. "And I still don't understand!"

Emma took a deep breath. "I think you're overreacting. What's the difference whether I'm in Africa or back at school at Goucher?"

"About five thousand miles," Kurt said. "Give or take a few thousand."

Emma bit her lip and stared plaintively at her boyfriend. She remembered when they'd first started to get to know each other and she'd told him about her dreams of going to Africa, maybe even to work with primates like Jane Goodall. *He was so supportive of me then,* Emma thought wistfully.

"Please, Kurt, I need you to understand."

Kurt glanced back over at the kids in the pool, then his gaze returned to Emma. "I'm trying," he told her. "It just . . . it feels like you're choosing the Peace Corps over me."

"Oh, no!" she assured him. "It won't make any difference in how I feel about you. I love you and I always will. No matter where I am."

"Emma, no offense, but you don't know how you'll feel about me if you're on the other side of the world. We'll never see each other. It's tough to stay in love with a memory."

"But that's not how it will be!" Emma exclaimed. "I have it all figured out. You'll come visit me!"

"Yeah, right," Kurt replied, "I have about three or four thousand dollars lying around for plane tickets to Tanzania."

"I'll bring you over," Emma offered. "That's not a problem, Kurt."

Kurt grimaced. "You know I hate for you to spend your money—your family's money—on me."

"But—" Emma began.

"You can stay in a fool's paradise or you can face reality," Kurt said gruffly. "If you go, it's going to turn us upside down."

Emma was quiet for a moment. "I don't believe that."

"You want to have your cake and eat it, too," Kurt said. "Maybe you think you can because you've always had everything handed to you—"

"Kurt! That is so unfair—"

Kurt grabbed Emma's arm. "Okay, it's unfair. The whole thing is damned unfair! Frigging life is unfair!"

Tears came to Emma's eyes. "I won't stop loving you. I don't know what to say to get you to believe that."

She looked at Kurt's sad face and she longed

to do something to comfort him. *I love him so much,* she thought. *Am I sure that I'm doing the right thing? What's my hurry?*

Kurt spoke up again, and it was as if he had read her mind. "Why don't you just wait until you're done with college? Why do you have to go now?" he asked.

"Because I don't care about college right now," Emma answered. "Because the thought of going back to that school with those other rich spoiled brats makes me sick! Because the idea of sitting in one more art history lecture makes my teeth hurt!"

This time, Kurt was silent.

"You've got your heart set on this, don't you?" he said in a sad voice.

Emma murmured yes.

"Do you know what you're getting yourself into?" he asked, fighting for control of his voice. "They don't have insect repellent where you're going."

Emma offered him a tremulous smile.

Kurt touched her hair softly. "It means a lot to you, doesn't it?"

"Kurt," Emma said, "it's what I really want to do. Why shouldn't I try to do what I really want to, if I can? Why should I wait? What's the point?"

"Have you applied yet?" Kurt asked.

"I'm filling out the application tonight with

Carrie," Emma said. "It's really involved, and Jane told me they're very selective. But one of the heads of the Peace Corps is a friend of the Hewitts so that might help."

"That's convenient," Kurt muttered.

"I've still got to be approved," Emma said, ignoring Kurt's remark. "And usually you have to be a college graduate."

"So you might not get in," Kurt said, his voice full of hope.

"I'm determined," Emma said firmly. "I think there's a really good chance."

Kurt smiled sadly at Emma. "Who could ever turn you down?"

Emma smiled back at him. She loved him so much, and he really was trying to help.

"Anyway, you wouldn't leave until the fall, right?"

"Right," Emma said, feeling hopeful for the first time since she'd approached Kurt. *He's really trying to understand,* she thought to herself. *There is no other guy in the world like him.*

Then Kurt got a distant look in his eyes, and a small smile played around his lips.

"What?" Emma asked him.

"Oh, nothing," he said with exaggerated innocence.

The odd look in Kurt's eyes was still there.

"You don't look like it's nothing," Emma said.

"Well," Kurt replied, "maybe it's something.

21

And then again, maybe it isn't."

Emma put her hands on her hips. "What is that supposed to mean?"

"It means . . . just remember—because you think you're going to join the Peace Corps now doesn't mean nothing could possibly happen that could change your mind."

"Well, that's pretty cryptic," Emma said.

"We'll see," Kurt replied, "we'll see. Anyway, I'm allowed to lobby to keep you here, right?"

"You are," Emma answered, "so long as if I tell you to stop, you stop."

Kurt stuck out his hand. "You've got a deal, partner. You've got a deal."

"Have you ever engaged in any intelligence activities for the United States Government or any other government?" Carrie read the question from the application to Emma, as the two of them lay sprawled on the floor of Emma's room upstairs at the Hewitt house.

Emma grinned. "Do I look like a spy?" she asked.

"Actually," Carrie replied, "it's always the ones you never figure—"

"We can mark 'no' for that one," Emma said.

"And then we need a medical history on you," Carrie said, continuing to read.

"That's easy. I'll fill that in later," Emma replied, peering over Carrie's shoulder.

"Then you need six personal references who can vouch for your character," Carrie announced.

"No problem," Emma responded. "You, Sam, Billy, Jane Hewitt, Graham Perry Templeton, and—"

"Diana De Witt," Carrie joked, mentioning the name of the girls' arch enemy on the island.

"I was thinking of Lorell Courtland," Emma cracked, naming the other girl who was always in either Emma, Sam, or Carrie's face.

"How about Flash Hathaway?" Carrie grinned. "Say cheese, babe!"

Emma and Carrie cracked up and rolled around on the floor in laughter. Flash Hathaway was a smarmy photographer who most recently had been assigned to photograph Flirting With Danger—the band for whom Emma and Sam sang back-up—on their big East Coast tour. Flash was known for chasing anything in a skirt.

"Yes," Emma said, in her most ladylike voice. "Place Flash Hathaway's name there."

"What about Kurt?" Carrie said, stifling her laughter.

"What about him?" Emma replied lightly.

"You didn't mention him as a reference," Carrie said reasonably. "You did tell him about this, right?"

"Today." Emma sighed.

"So? What was his reaction?"

"Weird," Emma said, "really weird." She told

23

Carrie about her poolside conversation with Kurt, and about the strange look he had gotten in his eyes at the end of the conversation.

"He's just afraid of losing you," Carrie said. "It's happened before."

"But I don't intend to break up with him," Emma stated.

"Look at it from his perspective," Carrie urged her friend. "He really, really cares for you, and—"

"And I'm going to another continent for two years," Emma concluded. "Well, we're just going to have to make it work. If we really have a strong relationship, it'll work, anyway. Don't you think?"

"I don't know. I'm glad it's not me. What's the next question?" Carrie asked.

Emma picked up the application. "Practical experience for Peace Corps Service is question number fifteen," she said. "Oh God, look at this."

Emma and Carrie bent their heads over the form. It said that Peace Corps programs were divided into general work categories, like food production and natural resources, business and engineering, skilled trades, and education teaching. Listed under each general work category were specialties such as animal husbandry, metalwork, youth work and coaching, and adult education. The form stated that applicants should list their level of experience in each area along with dates of involvement, and talk about their activities.

Emma sighed. "I don't qualify for any of this," she said, her heart sinking.

"Don't be so negative," Carrie said. "You sure you don't know anything about beekeeping or sanitary engineering?"

Emma managed a small smile. "Not much," she said. "I don't suppose caring for the Hewitt kids counts, huh?"

"That's definitely animal husbandry." Carrie smiled.

"Maybe I don't have any skills they'd want," Emma said.

"Well, you really do have lots of child care experience," Carrie pointed out. "You can put that down for youth work."

"The only other thing I know is languages," Emma said.

"Well, maybe there's a specialty in those." Carrie starting to flip through the pages of the form. "Look here! Question eighteen: List languages known or studied within the past ten years below."

Emma looked at the question. *There's still hope*, she thought. *I speak Spanish, French, German, and Italian fluently. Maybe I can teach those.*

Carrie looked at her watch. "God, I gotta get

out of here. I told the Templetons I'd be home by eleven."

Emma said good-bye to her friend, walked her to the front door, and then went back upstairs to wrestle again with the Peace Corps application.

This isn't easy. Then she thought about what the two years she was going to face in Africa were going to be like, and she understood why the government hadn't made the application easy.

The application is a piece of cake compared to the experience, Emma thought. *I mean, I'm using an electric light to read this, and I'm not sure I'll have electricity there.*

She turned her attention back to the application. She decided to go back and fill out the practical experience section later. For now, she turned to the essay section:

MOTIVATION STATEMENT: While most Peace Corps Volunteers over the years have been positive about their overseas experiences, service in a developing country presents major physical, emotional, and intellectual challenges. Below, please provide a statement that includes:

1. your reasons for wanting to serve overseas as a Peace Corps Volunteer, and

2. how your reasons for wanting to serve

as a volunteer are related to your personal life goals and past activities.

Following the question were about forty blank lines in which to write an answer.

Emma sat on her bed and reread the question. Then she reached for a pen and some scrap paper, and began to write:

PEACE CORPS VOLUNTEER
MOTIVATIONAL STATEMENT
by Emma Cresswell

I had the good fortune to be born into one of the richest families in America. The biggest physical challenge for me growing up was deciding which ski run to take down which mountain in Switzerland. And yet in the past two years, I've come to understand that there are life experiences I long to have that all the money in the world can never buy. . . .

THREE

"Oh no," Kurt groaned, "it's a mime."

Emma swatted playfully at his hand on her waist. "Hey, there's nothing wrong with mimes! Mime is a very respected art form."

"I'm with Kurt," Billy said, walking hand-in-hand along the wharf with Carrie. "What kind of guy decides to make his living wearing tights and makeup?"

"A ballet dancer, for one," Carrie said pointedly. She watched the mime pretend he was stuck in a large box, feeling the air around him on all sides. "That's the oldest one in the book." She giggled. "It *is* pretty lame."

"Well, I disown all of you," Emma replied in mock indignation. "You're Philistines."

"You can't disown me," Kurt said, pulling her close and kissing her cheek. "You're crazy about me."

Emma snuggled closer to Kurt and grinned happily. Things were going so well it was scary. It was two days later, and she, Kurt, Billy, and

Carrie had all actually managed to find a couple of hours free to go on a picnic by the pier. They were casually strolling by the area where street musicians and artists of all kinds put on their shows for donations.

Ever since Emma had told Kurt that she was planning to join the Peace Corps at the end of the summer he'd been . . . well, he'd been fine. *That's what's so scary*, Emma thought. *I mean, at first he was so upset—just like I knew he'd be. But then he made those cryptic comments about trying to talk me out of it, and now he doesn't bring it up at all. He just acts happy. Very strange.*

"Oh, that's cute, look at that little girl tap dancing!" Carrie said, watching a dark-haired girl of about six tapping energetically to music blasting from a cassette player. Her thin, anxious-looking mother stood near her, obviously going through every one of her daughter's moves in her head.

"Smile, Melody!" the mother hissed.

The little girl obeyed and instantly slapped a wide smile on her face.

"Ugh, stage mother," Billy muttered. "There's nothing worse."

"You're completely wrong, man," Kurt said tersely.

Billy looked at him in surprise but didn't say anything.

The little girl finished on one knee, her arms

held out wide. The foursome clapped politely, and the child grabbed a battered-looking cap from her mother and passed it around for tips. The mother looked both embarrassed and proud as her daughter collected money from the small crowd. Suddenly Emma noticed a button missing on the woman's shirt. She noticed how thin both the girl and her mother were, and how the edges of the girl's obviously homemade costume were tattered.

Emma took a ten-dollar bill out of her purse and slipped it as unobtrusively as possible into the little girl's hat.

"Thank you!" the little girl said, her eyes wide. She collected from the rest of the crowd and ran back to her mother.

"I know them," Kurt told his friends as they walked away. "That little girl's father was a fisherman until two years ago when his arthritis got so bad that he couldn't fish anymore. They live in the poor part of town."

They all knew what Kurt was talking about. On the other side of the island there was a small but very real section of town where some poor families lived. Most of the rich summer tourists didn't even realize there were any poor people on elite Sunset Island. But Kurt, who had grown up on the island and loved it dearly, had shown his friends how those people lived. Kurt was active in COPE, Citizens of Positive Ethics, an organization trying to help the poor families on the island. Emma, Carrie, and Sam had joined too, and they sometimes did volunteer work for the group.

"Hey, I'm sorry about the remark before," Billy said to Kurt.

"It's okay," Kurt replied easily. "You didn't know."

Emma looked over at Kurt as they walked toward the beach. *He is the coolest*, she thought to herself. *He is the most sensitive guy I've ever met. Maybe he really has just decided to be understanding about my going to Africa. Maybe it really can work out.*

"This is a good spot," Carrie decided, dropping her picnic basket on the sand.

They spread out the old quilt they'd brought with them and fell on it, stretching out under the beautiful afternoon sun.

"Mmmmm, this is heavenly, there's even a breeze," Emma said, settling her head in Kurt's lap and closing her eyes. He stroked her hair tenderly.

"Okay, we've got tuna grinders, veggie grinders, or everything-but-the-kitchen-sink grinders," Carrie said, digging into the basket of food. She'd picked up grinder sandwiches on her way to meet her friends. Emma had made dessert, Billy brought chips and Cokes, and Kurt had made a huge salad.

"Veggie for me, please," Emma said, sitting up.

Carrie passed out the sandwiches, everyone dug plastic forks into Kurt's salad, and they ate happily for awhile.

"This sandwich is huge," Emma said, taking dainty bites of the giant sub.

"Yeah, it's Sam-sized," Carrie joked.

Emma nibbled on a tomato slice. "Do you think she's okay? I mean, now that she's broken up with Pres?"

Billy's face hardened. "Sam's always okay." He took a long drink from his Coke.

"I don't think that's true," Carrie said contemplatively. "I think she's not nearly as tough as she pretends to be."

"I don't know . . ." Billy said doubtfully.

"Maybe she just hasn't met the right guy yet," Kurt put in. He looked at Emma. "When you meet the right person, you know. And then you don't play games anymore."

Emma smiled at Kurt. *He is the right person for me,* she thought to herself. *I know it deep in my heart. I know we've had some problems, like when Kurt actually slept with Diana De Witt last summer—God, I thought I'd die of a broken heart. I never thought we'd get back together after that. And then there was Adam in California—I fell for him so hard, so fast. . . . But I feel more mature now, more ready to commit to—*

"Hey, who wants to play Frisbee?" Billy called out, startling Emma out of her reverie. He jumped up with a Day-Glo green Frisbee in his hands.

"I'm too full," Emma said, laying back down on the blanket.

"Yeah, me, too," Kurt agreed lazily.

"Oh, sure," Billy said with a laugh. "You two just want to lay around and suck face. Okay, Car, it's me and you!"

Billy and Carrie ran near the edge of the water and began tossing the Frisbee to each other. For a while, Emma and Kurt watched them, laying side by side on their stomachs. Then Kurt rolled over and put his arm around Emma.

"Did you hear what he accused us of?" he asked indignantly. He brushed some hair off Emma's face.

"Horrid," Emma replied, turning on her side to face Kurt.

"Yeah, horrid," Kurt agreed in a low voice. He leaned over and kissed her gently. Emma put her arms around him and kissed him back. The kiss turned more passionate as Kurt held Emma closer, their bodies touching from face to toes. Emma could feel the heat emanating from Kurt. She loved that he wanted her so much—it was both delicious and scary. Finally, she pulled away and rolled over on her back. Kurt rolled over, too.

"Yeah, take five or they're gonna have to come hose us down," Kurt joked, his voice ragged.

"You always feel so good," Emma murmured, staring up at the bright, blue sky.

"I can't make you feel that good if you're on the other side of the world," Kurt said quietly.

Emma turned her head to look at him. It was the very first time he'd brought up her plans since she'd told him about the Peace Corps. "Kurt, I—"

"I know, you've made up your mind," he said softly, looking at her with a small smile. "But sometimes even a person who has made up her mind changes it. It's not illegal."

"No, it's not illegal," Emma said quietly.

"Just remember, sweet Emma," he said, reaching for her again, "never say never."

And then she couldn't say anything, because he was kissing her again.

"She's late," Carrie said, looking at her watch.

"She's always late," Emma pointed out, "but she always shows up eventually."

It was evening now. They sat on a bench near the entrance to the new miniature golf course, Island Tees, waiting for Sam to show up. The unique course featured abstract sculptures, waterfalls, and artistic labyrinths. It was lit by various colored floodlights, and New Age music played through the large speakers.

After the picnic, Emma had taken Ethan to his diving lesson, driven Katie to a play date, and picked up some groceries for dinner. Then she'd helped cook, serve, and clean up, and then she'd bathed Katie, read her a story, and put her to bed. Frankly, she was glad to be out of the house.

"Kurt didn't seem too upset this afternoon about your leaving in the fall," Carrie remarked.

"He's acting very strange," Emma said. "I keep feeling like something's up."

"Like what?" Carrie asked, digging her putter into the dirt at her feet.

Emma shrugged. "I don't know. It's like he has some kind of secret. I mean, I'm glad he's not pouting, but . . ."

"But something isn't right," Carrie finished for her.

Emma shook her head. "Listen to me! I'm complaining because he *isn't* upset. I must be crazy."

"Hossanahs, you fellow foxes!" Sam called, running toward them from the parking lot. "Am I late?"

"Is the pope Catholic?" Carrie asked.

"Well, sorry, but this time it wasn't my fault," Sam said. "I couldn't leave until Mr. Jacobs got home from his date with his latest companion. This one's name is Arlette—she came home with him. Arlette is a student at Bangor Beauty Academy, she was proud to inform me. She offered to do my hair."

Carrie and Emma looked up at their friend. "It looks like you took her up on it."

Sam's wild red hair had been plaited into a dozen braids all over her head. "It's kind of cool, don't you think?" She whirled around for her friends, and the braids flew in all directions.

Emma had to laugh. Sam was so . . . well, so Sam. In addition to her bizarre hairdo, she was wearing a teeny, tiny pink baby's T-shirt stretched over her small-busted frame, raggedy cut-off jeans with peace symbols painted on the legs, and her trademark red cowboy boots. Carrie had on baggy jeans, an oversized Yale T-shirt, and a Mets baseball cap. Emma looked down at herself in perfect white jeans and a crisp white cotton shirt that bared her tanned stomach.

"We got your putter for you," Carrie told Sam, handing it to her.

"Thanks," Sam said. She looked around at the art work that served as the golf course. "Mondo bizarro, huh?"

"It's different, all right," Emma agreed as they walked toward the first tee.

"Hold the phone," Sam said, staring up at the huge neon sign that read "ISLAND TEES." Next to the logo was a giant bikini-clad neon woman winking at a giant neon guy in surfer Jams. "Now, what is wrong with this picture? We've got the artsy, hi-tone golf course, and the too-hip music, and then there's a cartoon like that?"

Emma and Carrie looked at Sam blankly.

"Well, it's ugly, but so what?" Emma asked.

"Don't you get it?" Sam asked. "'Island Tees'? It's supposed to be a play on 'Island Tease.'"

Carrie and Emma looked up at the sign again.

"You think?" Carrie asked. "That never even occurred to me."

"I don't think, I know," Sam replied with disgust.

"Well, it's tasteless," Emma said with a shrug. "So what?"

"Besides, you're the biggest island tease I know!" Carrie said with a laugh.

"Well, you know my motto: so many guys, so little time," Sam said airily. "But that's not the point. The point is you don't see a sexy guy playing the tease in the stupid logo, do you? It's sexist."

"Well, we'll be sure to protest right after we play," Emma said, walking over to set her ball on the first tee. It led into a white abstract sculpture lit by pink floodlights. Emma planted her feet and hit the ball. It traveled through the center of the sculpture and landed on what would be the green—in this case it was white felt, to match the art project that was the first hole. The ball rolled to within two inches of the hole.

"Beginner's luck," Carrie called to Emma, setting up her shot. "I happen to be the miniature golf champion of—"

"Oh, my God," Sam hissed. She ran to Emma and attempted to hide behind her, which was tough considering that Emma was five inches shorter than her.

"What?" Emma asked, looking behind her.

"Don't be so obvious!" Sam whispered frantically.

And then Emma saw what Sam had seen. There was Pres just getting off his motorcycle in the parking lot. And with him was none other than Diana De Witt.

"I knew it, I knew it, I knew it," Sam moaned. "I knew he always really wanted her. Oh, I hate her, and I hate him, and I feel like jumping into the middle of that stupid sculpture so they won't see me."

"Sam, they're going to see you," Emma pointed out. "Just act dignified, as if you don't care."

Emma edged over to Carrie, leaving Sam standing with her head down. The three girls stood there together as Pres and Diana came closer. Diana saw them first. She grinned like the cat who ate the canary.

"Well, it's the Two Musketeers plus one bovine creature," Diana sang out.

Sam straightened up and faced Diana and Pres.

"Gee, small world," she said, looking Pres in the eye.

"Hey, Sam," Pres said quietly.

Diana took Pres' arm proprietarily. "Pres is going to show me his strokes," she said huskily.

"I bet," Sam spat out.

Diana took in Sam's braids. "Nice hairdo," she said sarcastically. "Your head has an attractive skull-like appearance."

Sam ignored Diana and kept her eyes glued to Pres' face. "Didn't anyone ever tell you that a person is known by the company he keeps?" she asked him.

"Which is exactly why he's no longer dating you!" Diana said with a malicious laugh.

Emma looked from Sam to Pres and back to Sam. They couldn't seem to take their eyes off each other. *They still love each other,* she realized. *It's so sad that Pres broke up with Sam. All he wanted was a commitment, and she just couldn't seem to make one. . . .*

"Have fun with your golf game," Pres told Sam, a steely look in his eyes.

"*We* certainly plan to have fun tonight," Diana insinuated. She rubbed up against Pres seductively. "It's such a *hot* night, don't you think?"

"Suddenly I don't feel much like playing," Sam said in a small voice. She dropped her club and ran away.

Emma and Carrie looked at each other.

"You're a bitch, Diana," Carrie said, and they hurried after Sam.

"Bye-bye, kiddies!" Diana called to them in a mocking voice.

"Oh, shut up," Emma heard Pres say to Diana as she and Carrie hurried after Sam. "Just shut up for once."

Hours later, Emma lay in her bed, unable to sleep. *Poor Sam,* she thought. *She's so miserable. I've never seen her cry like that before.* She and Carrie had done everything they could to comfort their friend, but Sam had still been miserable.

"Why was I such a fool?" she kept asking them. "I had the greatest guy in the world, and now I've lost him just because I couldn't stop myself from being such a stupid flirt. I hate myself!"

A little shiver of fear ran down Emma's spine. *I won't lose Kurt by going into the Peace Corps,* she told herself. *It's a completely different situation. I'm not a flirt, and I am ready to make a commitment!*

Still, she tossed and turned, feeling threatened by Sam's break-up with Pres. She punched her pillow, threw off the covers, and tried to sleep.

Thwack!

Emma opened her eyes. Had she heard something?

Thwack! Thwack!

She had *definitely* heard something. Something

at the window. Cautiously she padded to the window and looked down.

Thwack!

A pebble hit the windowpane.

There was Kurt, in the backyard, looking up.

She opened the window and stuck her head out. "What are you doing?" she whispered. "It's the middle of the night!"

"'What light through yonder window breaks?'" Kurt said dramatically, reciting from *Romeo and Juliet*.

Emma stifled a laugh and looked down at the guy she loved. "You have really lost your mind," she called to him softly.

"Come down!" he urged her.

She looked at herself. She was wearing a T-shirt of Kurt's that she'd stolen from him at the beach one day and a pair of pink silk bikini panties. "I'm not dressed!" she said giddily.

"Good!" Kurt called back happily.

She knew she should get dressed, or at least get a robe—what if the Hewitts or one of the kids woke up?—but somehow she felt daring and reckless, a far cry from the prim and proper girl she'd been when she'd first met Kurt the summer before. She hurried downstairs clad only in the over-sized T-shirt and panties. *God, I love him so much,* she thought.

She ran into his waiting arms and he scooped her up, whirling her around. Then he kissed her passionately until she was breathless.

"You're really crazy," she told him, hugging him fiercely. "I can't believe you did this!"

"Ah, this is not a precedent-setting move," Kurt reminded her. "Remember last summer?"

Emma smiled at the memory. Kurt was right. It was when they had first fallen in love. She had kept her wealthy and privileged background a secret, and when Kurt found out, he was really angry with her. They'd made up when he'd come to the house and thrown pebbles up at her window. That was the first time he'd ever told her he loved her.

"I remember," Emma whispered, burying her face in his fragrant, masculine-smelling neck.

He pulled away from her and gazed lovingly at her face. "God, you are so beautiful," he murmured.

"Oh, Kurt . . ." She kissed him with all the love that was in her heart.

"Emma . . ." he began. He stared at her, tears in the corners of his eyes. Then before she knew what was happening, he dropped his arms from around her and got down on one knee.

"What are you doing?" she asked him. "Reciting more Shakespeare?"

"Emma . . ." Kurt began again, gazing up at her.

She shivered a little in her T-shirt and rubbed at her arms. "Yes, Sir Galahad." She giggled.

"Am I supposed to knight you?"

But Kurt's face was very serious. "Emma Cresswell, I love you very much, and I will love and honor you forever," he said.

Emma's heart began thudding in her chest. Her eyes grew huge and her hands began to shake as realization dawned on her. *Oh, my God,* she thought. *Oh, my God, he's going to . . .*

Kurt took her hand and kissed it. "Emma, my love, will you marry me?"

FOUR

"Kurt *what*?" Sam demanded.

"He asked me to marry him," Emma repeated to Sam and Carrie.

"*Kurt asked you to marry him*?" Sam screeched.

"Shhhh!" Emma admonished, looking around at the curious faces of the other lunchtime diners at the Bay View Restaurant. "You don't have to tell the entire world!"

"Wow," Carrie breathed. "This is big!"

"First comes love, then comes marriage—" Sam sang out.

"Cut it out!" Emma warned Sam.

"But aren't you psyched?" Sam asked. "Why are you pulling one of your patented Cresswell-type ice looks on me?"

"Sam's right," Carrie said, her eyes shining happily. "This is just incredible! I mean, I knew Kurt was serious—but marriage!"

"I was even more shocked when he asked me last night than the two of you are right now," Emma said.

"Well, looks like you're the first of us to go," Sam said breezily. "And in between my wild trips with various rich and famous stud-puppets, I will look forward to visiting you two in your cozy split level in the burbs of Cleveland—"

"Cleveland?" Carrie asked.

"Oh, let's call it Good Ole Boring Anywhere, U.S.A.," Sam decided.

"That's not fair," Carrie defended Emma. "Just because a couple is married doesn't mean they have to become boring."

"Says who?" Sam asked. "You've met my parents?"

Carrie nodded her head.

"And you have parents?" Sam continued. Carrie nodded again.

"I rest my case," Sam said emphatically.

"But my parents aren't—" Carrie started to protest.

"Hey, wait a second," Emma interrupted, trying to get a word in edgewise. "You two seem to have overlooked something. I didn't say I said yes last night."

Carrie and Sam looked at Emma in stunned silence. As usual, it was Sam who spoke up first.

"You didn't?" Sam queried.

"You didn't?" Carrie echoed. "Wait a second, of course you didn't. You weren't even ready to get engaged-to-be-engaged, really. I just got carried away with the whole romantic fantasy of the thing."

"I didn't exactly say no, either," Emma added.

"You didn't?" Sam asked.

"You didn't?" Carrie echoed.

"It's not that simple," Emma tried to explain.

"What's not simple?" Sam pressed on. "He asked you—you have two options: yes or no. Which one was it?"

"No—" Emma answered quietly.

"But you just said—" Sam began.

"—for today," Emma continued. "I told Kurt no last night—it was the hardest thing I ever did—but he asked me to just think about it for another day before giving him an answer, and I said I would."

"That's my girl," Sam replied, taking a bite of bread. "Keep 'em hanging."

Carrie looked closely at Emma. "You must have been really shocked when he asked you," she said. "Was this because you told him you were going into the Peace Corps? Did he do it to try to get you not to go?"

"That's what I've been trying to figure out all day," Emma admitted, pushing a lettuce leaf around on her plate.

"What's the biggie?" Sam asked. "He either did or he didn't."

"Well," Emma started to explain, "at first he

said that if I said yes, he hoped we could make a home together here—"

"At least it's not Kansas," Sam cracked.

Emma ignored her. "But then I told him that it didn't matter, that I was going to go to Africa in the fall anyway."

"So that was that," Carrie surmised, taking a sip of water.

"No!" Emma cried. "Because then he said it didn't matter to him, all that was important was that we be together forever, even if I had to go Africa and do what I wanted there."

"Wow," Carrie marveled. "He said he didn't care if you were away from him for two years, so long as you were married?"

"Something like that," Emma admitted. "He said something about 'a spiritual connection forever.'"

"Spiritual connection. Where do I throw up?" Sam joked.

"I think that's so romantic." Carrie sighed.

"But I still told him no." Emma continued to push her lettuce leaf around.

"How did he react?" Carrie asked her.

"Better than you'd think," Emma said.

"He didn't have a fit?" Sam asked. "Because you know Kurt has a temper—"

"Nope," Emma answered. "He just said that he wished I would think it over some more before I gave him a final answer. And it was important

47

that I know he would support my going to Africa no matter what."

"Do you think . . . ?" Carrie began slowly. "Well, do you think he's kind of trying to manipulate you? You know, make you feel guilty enough to say yes?"

"I just don't know," Emma admitted. "I mean, I know Kurt loves me. I don't think anyone could ever love me any more than he loves me—"

"I sense a 'but' coming up here," Sam said, dipping a french fry in some ketchup.

"But I'm not ready to get married," Emma finished.

"Amen," Sam pronounced. "Here's to single babe-hood forever." She solemnly raised her glass. Then, seeing that neither Emma nor Carrie were raising theirs, she shrugged and drained her iced tea.

"Hey, you were awfully upset just yesterday about losing Pres to be so cool about being single forever today," Carrie reminded her.

"Well, that was yesterday. It was temporary insanity," Sam quipped.

Her friends just stared at her, not buying her explanation.

"Okay, okay," Sam muttered. "So I might be the teensiest bit in love with Pres, and my heart might be the teensiest bit broken. Don't rub it in."

"That's honest, at least," Carrie told her.

"Let's not talk about me," Sam suggested, popping the last french fry in her mouth. "Let's talk about Emma. Her life is, I am sorry to admit, more exciting."

"You're temporarily off the hook," Carrie told Sam. She turned to Emma. "I think you made a smart decision."

"I don't know," Emma mused. "It seems smart to me now, but—"

"So when will you see the spurned Romeo again?" Sam teased.

"This afternoon," Emma answered, glancing at her watch to see how much more time she had before she had to go pick up Katie Hewitt from her friend Emily's house. "He called this morning and asked me if he could come over. He said he could be very persuasive in person."

"I bet," Sam agreed, wiggling her eyebrows at Emma. "But somehow I think your employers will frown when he throws you down on their front lawn and tears your clothes off."

Emma laughed. "Sometimes it's me tearing his clothes off."

"Do you think there's a chance you'll change your mind?" Carrie asked.

Emma stared down at her uneaten salad. Her stomach felt all tied up in knots. "No," she finally said. "I won't change my mind."

"He's gonna be really, really disappointed," Sam warned Emma.

Emma sighed. "I just have to find a way to say no and still have him believe how much I love him."

"Right," Carrie agreed, but the look on her face said she didn't know if such a thing were possible.

"I'm not ready to get married," Emma repeated fervently, "but I'll die if I lose him."

"You won't lose him, Em," Sam said kindly.

"Right," Carrie agreed.

Emma managed a small smile. "I just hope I'm not about to do the worst thing in the world."

"What's that?" Carrie asked.

"To throw love away," Emma said softly. "Throwing love away."

Emma sat on the front porch of the Hewitts' house in the late afternoon sun, a book in her lap, waiting for Kurt. While she'd spent the afternoon doing her usual au pair work with the Hewitt kids, her mind had been a million miles away, mulling over the last thing she had said to Carrie and Sam at lunch.

Am I throwing love away? she thought to herself. *Am I doing something I'm going to regret the rest of my life? And if I change my mind and say yes, is that going to be something I'm going to regret?*

She closed her eyes and thought about when she'd been a little girl and had fantasies about growing up and falling in love. She could see her little five-year-old self, immaculately groomed per her mother's instructions, playing alone with an expensive bride doll she'd received for Christmas. She'd played wedding with the doll over and over again. In her fantasy, the doll was her, Emma grown up, marrying the handsomest man in the world, and they would live happily ever after.

Emma opened her eyes and stared out at the front yard. *I never thought about having a career, or what would happen if I fell in love too soon, or if the career and the handsome man didn't fit together,* she realized. *I thought true love would just be simple and forever. God, I'm so confused.*

She wished this was something she could talk about with her mother. *Oh, sure,* she snorted to herself. *Kat can't even deal with having a daughter who looks old enough to date, much less one who could be contemplating marriage.*

Then she thought about her Aunt Liz, her mother's younger sister and her favorite relative in the whole world. But even as she thought about confiding in her aunt, she knew that she had to confront Kurt with this tonight. She couldn't just keep him waiting. She had to tell him the truth: she just wasn't ready to be married.

Emma glanced at her watch: 5:15 P.M. Kurt had called her earlier to tell her that he had to take his car in for repairs, and that the Sunset Motors service department told him they would give him a loaner until his car was ready.

"It's bright red," Kurt had said. "Easy to spot. I'll stop by around 5:15."

Emma's stomach growled. She'd been so nervous about this all day that she hadn't eaten a thing. From time to time, she peered down the driveway, watching for Kurt's car. Because of how the driveway was situated, Emma had a clear view up the street for perhaps a tenth of a mile.

I'd like to get some warning on his arrival, Emma thought to herself. *If I catch an early glimpse of him coming, I'll try to calm myself down. My heart is pounding, my hands are clammy, I feel like throwing up. Why, oh why does this have to be so hard when we love each other so much?*

Emma looked up again from the book she was trying to read.

There it is! she said to herself.

A bright red Nissan Maxima was heading down Seagate toward the Hewitts', and Emma could see that Kurt was driving it.

Okay, time for five deep breaths, Emma thought.

Then something happened that Emma would not forget for the rest of her life.

As Kurt was slowing to approach the Hewitts'

driveway, another car—Emma couldn't see exactly what kind it was—came barreling around the curve in front of the Hewitts' house in the opposite direction.

Emma watched, horror-stricken.

The car had taken the curve too fast and was on Kurt's side of the road.

There was the squeal of brakes, as both Kurt and the other driver slammed their feet on their respective brake pedals.

Oh, my God, Emma thought, *they're going to—*

There was a sickening impact as the two cars collided head-on.

Emma screamed.

And then there was silence, except for the hissing of fluids from broken pipes and tubes from the two cars.

Emma screamed again. Then she ran toward the cars as fast as she could. Behind her, Jane and Jeff Hewitt came running out of the house—they had heard the collision. From far away, Emma could already hear the sounds of sirens—Jeff had immediately called 911 to alert emergency services.

Oh, God, Emma thought as she ran, *he's gone, he's dead. It was a head-on collision. No one survives head-on collisions. It could have been different. If I had told him yes, then we would have just met at the Play Café or somewhere, and this would never have happened. How could I be so stupid? He's going to be gone forever, and I'm going to be here all alone without him. I was stupid, stupid, stupid . . .*

Emma ran toward Kurt's crumpled car, wailing and crying. She saw that the driver's-side car door had been smashed open by the crash.

He's dead, she thought, running toward the car. *He's dead, and I can't live without him. Oh, God, how could you do this to him? How could you do this to me? Oh, Kurt, my darling, my love . . .*

Before she could reach the car, Emma fainted.

FIVE

Voices were talking to Emma, but she ignored them, as she lay on the road near the two mangled vehicles.

God, why are you being so cruel to me? Emma thought, as she slowly came awake. *Why are you doing this to me? I saw him die there, I saw it with my own eyes. Why are you putting his face in front of my eyes?*

"Emma, wake up," a gentle male voice said to her.

"Get up, Emma," a female voice said, which she recognized as Jane Hewitt's.

Emma recognized smelling salts being cracked under her nose. She came awake.

There were four people looking down at her: A paramedic. Jane and Jeff Hewitt. And Kurt Ackerman.

This can't be, Emma thought, *I'm hallucinating. But he looks so real, could it really be . . . ?*

"Kurt?" she said, in a small voice.

The figure above her reached down to embrace her. And then Emma realized it was true.

It was Kurt. He was alive. Emma felt joy like she'd never felt in her life. She screamed again, but this time it was a scream of pure, unadulterated happiness.

"Thank you, God, oh, thank you!" Emma cried, jumping to her feet and throwing her arms around Kurt.

"Thank God for air bags," Kurt observed. "Look at me. Not a scratch."

She looked him over, head to foot, feeling his chest with her hands. "Really? You're really okay? Oh, I can't believe it!"

"I'm right here," Kurt told her, cradling her gently in his arms.

"That's the most scared I've ever been in my life," Emma gulped out. "It was even worse than when my father had the heart attack—"

"Shhhh, it's okay now," Kurt promised.

Emma pulled away and looked around. "The other driver—?"

"Had an air bag, too. He's fine," Kurt assured her. "We can be in a TV commercial together, now."

"I'm so glad you're—"

"Me, too," Kurt whispered, "me, too."

A wave of emotion poured over Emma, and so did a million thoughts. *I was going to risk spending my life without him. But I just saw what life*

*would be like without him. Was God giving me
the sign that I was looking for? Am I really ready
to risk being without Kurt? He's the greatest guy
in the world!*

"Kurt?" Emma whispered.

"Yes?" Kurt answered, still holding her.

"I changed my mind," Emma said tremulously.
"I will marry you."

"That is the most unbelievable story I've ever
heard in my life," Carrie said, hugging her knees
to her chest. She dug her toes into the sand.
"Kurt and the other driver are so lucky they
had air bags!"

The three girls sat together on a blanket on the
beach in the moonlight. Emma had just recounted
the story of what had happened that very afternoon.

"It could be a movie," Sam marveled, "a made-
for-TV movie."

"Of course, you'd star in it," Carrie joked.

"Yeah, we'd just change Emma to a bodacious
redhead," Sam decided.

"It must have been so hard to tell Kurt you
weren't going to marry him after that," Carrie
mused.

"Well, that's just it," Emma said slowly. She
looked from Carrie to Sam. "I said yes."

"No!" Sam squeaked.

"I really did," Emma said. "I saw what life

would be like without Kurt, and I just couldn't bear it. So I said yes!"

"That's . . . that's just incredible!" Carrie exclaimed.

"I can't believe it myself," Emma agreed. "I mean, I had no intention—"

"Of saying yes?" Carrie asked.

"Right," Emma said. "But I did."

"And you meant it?" Sam asked.

"Of course I meant it," Emma replied. "With all my heart."

"But . . . but you were so set on the fact that you're not ready to get married," Carrie reminded her gently.

"I know," Emma said softly. She stared out at the dark ocean and shivered a little in the night air. "But it was a sign. I saw what life would be like without him, and that's when I realized . . ."

"What?" Sam asked expectantly.

"That I'm meant to be with Kurt. I love him so much."

Carrie hesitated a moment. "Well, then we're happy for you. Right, Sam?"

"Right," Sam agreed.

They were all silent for a moment.

"You, married," Sam mused. "It doesn't seem real."

"I know," Emma said.

"I still feel like such a kid," Sam continued.

"So do I," Emma said with a laugh.

"But then how can you be getting married?"

Emma grinned. "I'm a kid in love." She jumped up. "I've got a surprise in the car. Be right back."

Emma ran to the Hewitts' car and got out the bottle of champagne the Hewitts had given her when they heard her say yes to Kurt's proposal. They told her to share it with Carrie and Sam when she told them, and that's just what she was about to do. She grabbed the fluted glasses she'd borrowed and hurried back to her friends.

"It's time to celebrate!" Emma called as she ran toward Carrie and Sam.

"Ooo, champagne on the beach—illegal and decadent!" Sam noted gleefully, taking a glass from Emma.

"Well, if you can't have a glass of champagne the day you get engaged, then life is a sorry thing," Emma pronounced. She smoothly opened the bottle of champagne, which offered a small *pop*, and poured a little into each of the three glasses.

"A toast!" Sam said, jumping to her feet. She looked down at Carrie and Emma. "Stand up, girlfriends! This is our first wedding toast ever!"

Emma and Carrie stood up, and all three girls held out their glasses.

"To Emma Cresswell, Boston Ice Princess—and vestal virgin!—who will not be a virgin for very much longer, I might add—but who, whether single, married, divorced, or Martian, will always be our best friend," Sam pronounced.

"Hear hear!" Carrie cried.

The girls clinked glasses and drank.

"L'chaim," Sam said, and she took a large swallow of the champagne. "That means 'to life' in Hebrew," she translated.

"I want to do one, too," Emma demanded.

"You're not supposed to toast yourself at your own engagement!" Carrie said with a laugh. "What would Emily Post say?"

"What would Kat Cresswell say?" Sam added solemnly. She turned to Emma. "Oh, God, you're actually going to have to tell your mother."

"I refuse to think about my mother at this moment," Emma announced. "Now . . ." She cleared her throat.

Oh, please, I can't believe I'm getting tears in my eyes and a lump in my throat, she thought as she prepared to speak.

"Well?" Sam urged her. "The champagne is getting warm!"

"Sam, shut up," Carrie said cheerfully.

"I just wanted to say," Emma began, "that I'm really happy that I'm getting to spend this night with my two best friends in the entire world."

"Where's Kurt?" Sam cracked.

"Hey, I've got more!" Emma exclaimed. "And that we will be friends forever . . . and that I'm looking forward to proposing the toast when you each announce your engagements," Emma finished.

"Don't hold your breath," Sam said. "I haven't even got a boyfriend, and I don't think I *ever* want a husband."

"Well, I do," Carrie said. "Maybe," she added tentatively.

"Let's drink to maybe," Emma suggested.

"L'chaim," Carrie responded.

Emma and her friends sipped their champagne for the second time and plopped back down on the blanket on the sand.

I almost never drink, Emma reminded herself, *but this is really a special occasion!*

The three of them sat there together in silence, listening to the waves breaking over and over. It was a moonless night, and there were a million stars in the sky. Emma started timing her breaths to match the sound of the waves and thought back for the hundredth time on the amazing events of the afternoon.

"You're sure about this?" Carrie blurted out.

"Huh?" Emma said, pulling herself out of her reverie.

"I asked whether you were sure that you were sure?" Carrie repeated. "I mean, I don't want to put a damper on your happiness—"

"Totally," Emma said. She felt at peace. "I'm doing the right thing."

"So, you're sure," Carrie repeated.

"Why do you keep asking me that?" Emma wondered.

"I'm sorry," Carrie said. "It's just . . . you were so sure that you didn't want to . . ."

"Things change, right, Em?" Sam asked.

"Right," Emma said with finality.

"Well, then, cool," Sam said. "Have you picked a date?"

"Well, we've thought that—"

"Because I have to check my calendar for the next couple of years," Sam said. "I'm kinda busy."

Emma made a face at her friend. "We were sort of thinking that maybe in two weeks—"

"Two weeks?!" Sam exploded, kicking sand all over the place. "You can't plan a wedding in two weeks!"

Carrie moved closer to Emma. "Sam's right," she said. "There are a lot of details to take care of. Don't you think that's kind of soon?"

"It would be, but—"

"But what?" Sam demanded.

Emma grew quiet. This was one thing she didn't like to think about, and now that she was getting married, she didn't like to think about it even more.

"My father's going into the hospital for bypass surgery in three weeks," she muttered.

And thank goodness for that, Emma thought.

When he had that heart attack here on the island earlier this summer and nearly died, it was one of the worst times of my life!

Sam whistled. "Whoa, baby," she said. "When did you find this out?"

"A few days ago," Emma said. "I didn't really want to talk about it before. I was still getting used to the idea. But it seemed like a good thing, and the doctor said it was important."

"But why don't you wait until he's completely recovered?" Carrie wondered.

"Yeah," Sam agreed. "Give yourself time to plan the kind of wedding that the Cresswells of Boston can afford."

"It's really, really serious surgery," Emma said. "What if something goes wrong?"

For a moment, Emma had a horrible vision of her father back in the hospital, dying because of some stupid mistake during the bypass surgery.

"That's not going to happen," Carrie reassured her.

"So you want the wedding before . . ." Sam said.

"That's right," Emma agreed. "I want to make absolutely certain that my father can walk me down the aisle."

"Wow," Sam said, nodding. "Back in Kansas, when people get married, they start planning it like the decade before."

"Two weeks . . ." Carrie marveled.

"I'm going to have so much to do," Emma worried.

"Correction, Miss Ice Princess," Sam corrected her, pouring a bit more champagne into her glass, "*we've* got so much to do."

"But—"

"No buts." Sam cut her off. "There's no way you'll be able to get this done alone."

"Sam's right," Carrie said.

Emma thought about it for a moment and saw that it would absolutely be the right thing to do to enlist her friends.

"Okay," Emma agreed.

"Good!" Sam exclaimed. "First thing we'll do is hire Diana De Witt to do the ceremony—"

"—and Flash Hathaway as the official photographer!" Carrie added.

"Okay," Emma agreed, "but only if Lord Whitehead and the Zit People can play the wedding march!"

The three of them exploded into spasms of laughter. It actually took Emma a minute to catch her breath.

"So," Carrie asked, when the three of them had calmed down enough to talk again, "how much did you and Kurt get to talk about?"

"Not much," Emma admitted. "We talked for about an hour early this evening, but then he had to go to work."

"Good," Sam said regally. "Then it's all up to you."

"Sam!" Carrie scolded.

"Well," Emma said, "we did decide we wanted to write our own ceremony."

"Emma," Sam chided her, "this is the 1990s, not the 1960s. You don't write—"

"We are writing our own wedding vows and that is that," Emma stated emphatically.

"So, can I wear patchouli oil and a tie-dyed shirt?" Sam asked. "Seriously retro!"

"Who are you going to invite?" Carrie asked.

"Yeah, is that creep Austin Payne coming with your mother?" Sam asked.

Emma made a face. She hated Austin Payne, the young artist half the age of her mother, who her mother had been dating, and threatening to marry, for a couple of years. *Austin Payne is an officious jerk*, she thought.

Then she smiled, remembering that her mother and father, who had been embroiled in a hostile divorce settlement for what seemed like forever to Emma, appeared to be putting their relationship back together again, especially after Emma's father's heart attack.

"I doubt it," Emma said. "For all I know, my mother and father will walk me down the aisle together."

"If there is an aisle," Sam sniffed. "It'll probably be tie-dyed, too."

"This isn't getting us very far," Carrie said.

"There's a lot to do," Emma said softly.

"And we're not going to get it done tonight," Carrie noted. "So how about if we have a planning session tomorrow? When are we all free?"

The girls compared notes and decided to meet the next day, late in the afternoon, in the Hewitts' backyard.

"So for now, we party!" Sam shouted. "How about a swim?"

"*What?*" Carrie said with a laugh.

"A swim!" Sam said.

"We don't have bathing suits!" Emma yelped.

"We'll go as we are!" Sam chortled.

The girls looked at each other. They were all wearing shorts and T-shirts.

What the heck, Emma thought, *you only get married once . . . or at least, you should only get married once!*

"Last one in marries Flash Hathaway!" Sam screamed, and ran toward the ocean.

Emma and Carrie jumped up and followed her.

The three of them reached the waves at the same time and dived in, splashing and cavorting in the shallow water.

The night air was warm, the water was cold, and Emma thought she'd never been so happy in her entire life.

SIX

"I've been thinking about you all day," Kurt breathed sexily into the phone. "Do you know how fabulous you are?"

"No, I think you should tell me," Emma said with a laugh in her voice. She felt so happy. In just a few minutes, Carrie and Emma were coming over to help her plan her wedding. *My wedding!* she thought to herself. *Something I've dreamed about my entire life!*

"Well, let's see," Kurt mused. "You're moderately attractive, reasonably intelligent, somewhat interesting—if you like the speaks-five-languages-fluently type—"

"Ooh, tell me more," Emma cooed happily.

"Let's see . . . you've been known to be a halfway decent friend to your friends, and, uh, there must be more—oh yeah, you love me," Kurt finished.

"Gee, I really am irresistible," Emma agreed.

"I can't wait to see you tonight," Kurt said huskily.

"What time do you get off work?" Emma asked.

"I'm done teaching at the club at seven," Kurt said. "Then I'm gonna stop home to tell my dad and my sisters the big news. I should be over about nine, okay?"

"You're telling your family tonight?" Emma asked.

"Sure," Kurt replied easily. "This afternoon I asked Dad to get my mom's diamond ring out of the safe deposit box. I don't think this is gonna come as any big news to him."

"Oh, Kurt," Emma said tenderly.

He had told her that before his mom died of cancer she had given him her diamond ring and told him she wanted him to give it to the woman he loved when they got engaged. Kurt's dad kept it for him in the family's safe deposit box.

"What did your father say when you asked him?" Emma wondered.

"Well, I didn't exactly ask him," Kurt amended. "I spoke with my sister, Faith, and left him a message."

"Do you think he'll be upset?" Emma wondered.

"Nope," Kurt said firmly. "After how well you took care of your dad when he was so sick, my dad thinks you're pretty cool."

"Cool enough for you to marry?"

"He'll be lucky to have you for a daughter-in-law," Kurt replied. "When are you planning to tell your parents?"

"Oh, God," Emma groaned.

"Em, you have to call them," Kurt said. "Today."

"I know," Emma said with a sigh. "But you know my mother . . ."

"We're all grown up now, Em," Kurt said. "We don't have to have Mom and Dad's approval anymore."

"You're right. I know you're right," Emma said.

"Good. So, I'll see you about nine," Kurt reminded her. "I love you." He hung up.

Emma hung up the phone in the Hewitts' kitchen. She picked up the notebook she was using for her wedding plans and headed out into the backyard.

God, I have to tell my mother. She is going to have an absolute fit, Emma thought as she sat down at the redwood table. *She's going to kill me. Or lock me away for the millennium. Or something worse.*

"Hi, whatcha doing?" four-year-old Katie said, crawling up to sit next to Emma. She held her favorite raggedy doll, Sally, by one hand. The family dog (a mutt who was named, appropriately enough, Dog) had been following Katie around, and now he curled up contentedly at Emma's feet.

"Thinking," Emma told the little girl.

"About your wedding?" Katie asked, her eyes growing wide.

"Yes," Emma replied. "I have lots of work to do."

Katie's eyebrows drew together. "I didn't think you were old enough to get married," she said. "I thought you were still a kid."

"Well, I'm not," Emma said, ruffling Katie's hair.

"I didn't mean a little kid," Katie hastened to explain. "I mean, sheesh, I know you're a lot bigger than me. But my mommy didn't marry my daddy until she was twenty-six, and you're only . . . I forgot how old."

"Nineteen," Emma reminded her.

"Yeah," Katie agreed, sucking contemplatively on Sally's hand.

"Well, nineteen is old enough to get married," Emma explained.

"Oh." Katie reached down and scratched a mosquito bite on her leg. "So, do I get to go to the wedding?"

"Of course!" Emma cried. "In fact," she added impetuously, "how would you like to be the flower girl?"

Katie's eyes filled up her entire face. "Flower girl?"

Emma nodded. "You would wear a beautiful, special dress, and you'd be in the wedding. You'd come down the aisle and you'd carry lots of flowers in a basket."

"I could really be in the wedding?" Katie asked.

"Oh, yes," Emma said, hugging Katie. "It will be wonderful!"

Katie jumped off the table. "Come on, Dog!" she called to the family mutt. "We have to go tell Mommy we're in Emma's wedding!"

Emma smiled as the little girl ran into the house. *Now, if only my mother would have a similar reaction*, she thought. *I know I have to call her, but I'm dreading it. Maybe I'll call my father first in Florida . . .*

"I'm telling you, she will," Sam said, as she and Carrie rounded the corner into the Hewitts' backyard.

"No way," Carrie said. "She's too romantic to do that."

"You mean, she's too smart not to," Sam shot back.

"Well, hi," Emma called to them. "What are you two arguing about?"

"You," Sam said. She threw her purse on the table and flung her body into the nearby hammock. "I'll bet you ten bucks," she added to Carrie.

"You're on," Carrie replied, sitting next to Emma.

"Excuse me, did you two just bet ten bucks on

me?" Emma asked them.

"Wow, comfy hammock," Sam said, rocking with her eyes closed. "I may never go back to work."

"Hel-lo!" Emma called. "A bet? About me? Ten dollars?"

"She thinks she knows you better than I do, and she is wrong, wrong, wrong," Sam sang out.

"Could I be let in on this?" Emma asked.

"Sam thinks you're going to sleep with Kurt before the wedding night," Carrie said, "and I said that as long as you haven't slept with him in all this time, I was sure you'd be romantic enough to wait until you were married."

"So," Sam called out, "tell Carrie I'm right and let me collect my ten bucks."

"I can't believe you two are making bets about this!" Emma said.

Sam sat up. "Why not? You know I'm the nosiest person on the planet."

"How could I forget?" Emma asked dryly.

Sam walked over to Emma and sat on the other side of her. "I look at it this way. You wouldn't buy a new car before taking it for a test run, would you?"

Emma laughed. "Sam! Marriage is not like buying a new car!"

"Right, it lasts a lot longer—well, sometimes, anyway," Sam amended. "That's why I know you're gonna look under the old hood and take it for a drive before you purchase the merchandise."

Carrie looked at Emma. "She doesn't have a romantic bone in her body."

"All my bones are romantic," Sam said solemnly. She looked at Emma. "So, do I win my bet or not?"

Emma laughed. "Believe it or not, I haven't even given that a moment's thought."

Silence.

"Nay," Sam finally scoffed, "I don't believe it."

"I'm telling you the truth!" Emma exclaimed. "This is all happening so quickly that I . . . I don't know what I'm going to do."

"Don't you think it would be romantic to actually become lovers on your wedding night?" Carrie asked.

"Major yuck," Sam answered. "I mean, that line of thinking has never made any sense to me. One day it's 'oh, darling, we can't do it until we're married, it's wrong.' And then there's this magic ceremony and that night it's supposed to be 'hubba-hubba'!"

"You are a very strange person," Emma told her.

"Thank you," Sam said sweetly.

"Anyway, that's not what I meant," Carrie told Sam. "I'm not saying sex is wrong if you're not married—you know I don't feel that way. I'm just saying that if Emma and Kurt have waited all this time, what's another two weeks?"

"Uh, excuse me, but when you two are done figuring out my sex life, maybe we could actually work on planning the wedding?" Emma asked.

"That's what we're here for!" Sam said cheerfully. "So, what have you planned so far?"

They all moved down to the bench and stared at Emma's notebook.

"Uh, nothing," Emma admitted. "The notebook is empty."

"Nothing?" Carrie asked.

"Well, I took Katie to a play date this morning, and then I helped Jane do the laundry . . ." Emma looked at her friends. "No, that's not the real reason. The real reason is I get paralyzed every time I think about telling my mother."

"So, then, let's call her now," Sam suggested.

"Now?" Emma asked, panic in her voice.

"There's nothing she can do to you," Carrie reminded Emma.

"Cut me off without a cent," Emma mumbled.

Sam got a horrified look on her face. "No guy is worth that!"

"Oh, I'm kidding," Emma said. "I have lots of money in trust that I inherit when I'm twenty-five."

"Just out of curiosity," Sam asked slowly, "how much is lots?"

"Sam!" Carrie chided her. "That is so rude."

"I know," Sam agreed, "but I can't help myself. How much?"

"About twenty," Emma admitted.

"I have a feeling that isn't twenty dollars," Sam ventured. "Or even twenty thousand dollars."

Emma shrugged.

"Twenty million dollars?" Sam asked. "You're inheriting twenty million dollars?"

"Oh, I'll inherit a lot more than that when my parents die," Emma corrected her. "That's just my own trust fund."

Sam sighed. "I wish I could hate you, but I like you too much."

"Look, can we just change the subject, please?" Emma asked.

"Sure," Carrie said. "We can change it back to your calling your mother."

"No! I can't!" Emma shrieked.

"Come on!" Carrie coaxed her. "You usually enjoy giving your mother a heart attack or two!"

"I'll call my father first, how's that?" Emma decided. She climbed off of the bench, went inside for the cordless phone, and brought it back out with her. She pulled her little address book from her back pocket and looked up her father's number in Florida. Then she dialed the phone.

"Courage!" Carrie whispered, giving her arm a squeeze.

The phone rang three times, then her father's prerecorded voice came on the line.

"This is Brent Cresswell. Obviously I'm not free to take your call. Leave a message at the sound of the tone."

"Hi, it's Emma," she said. "Could you call me? Sometime soon? Thanks." She hung up the phone. "Well, I tried."

"So, call Kat," Sam said.

"Don't you think I should wait for my father to call me back first?" Emma asked meekly.

"Emma, you're planning to get married in two weeks," Carrie said. "You have no idea where your father even is today."

"You're right," Emma said. Even though her father's cardiologist had told him to slow down, and even though he said he planned to change his life—"take time to stop and smell the flowers" is what he'd told Emma—knowing the workaholic her father had always been, she doubted very much that he wasn't back at full throttle. *He might even be in Europe or Asia on business*, she realized. *I hope he phones in for his messages.*

Sam picked up the phone and handed it to Emma. "Bite the bullet."

Emma took the phone and dialed her mother's private number at the family's home on Beacon Hill in Boston. "It's ringing," she reported nervously to her friends.

"A good beginning," Sam cheered.

"Hello!" Kat Cresswell's gay voice came over the phone.

Emma gulped. "Hi, Mother, it's me." In all her life, she had never been able to call her mother "Mom," and certainly not "Kat," as her mother was constantly instructing her to do.

"Why, Emma, darling, how delightful to hear from you!" Kat cried.

"Yes, well, um . . . I wanted to, uh, talk with you," Emma began.

"You know, I was talking about you just today," Kat said cozily. "I was at my hairdresser while he did those blond-on-blond streaks he's been adding to my hair—summer highlights, you know—and I told him I wanted it just the color of yours!"

"Mine is natural," Emma said stiffly.

"Well, I know that, darling!" Kat agreed gaily. "But mine is just a tad darker, and you know how everyone says we look just like sisters!"

"Actually, you're the only one who says that," Emma replied icily. She immediately regretted it. First of all, it wasn't actually true—her mother was very beautiful and really did look young for her age. Second of all, she knew that it would just throw her mother into her "poor little girl" mode, which is exactly what happened.

"I just want you to think your mother is young and pretty," Kat said in her little-girl voice.

Emma gripped the phone hard. She could feel Carrie and Sam staring at her, and she took a deep breath and prayed for self-control. "I'm sorry I said that, Mother. It was mean."

"You love to wound me, Emma," her mother said. "I don't know why."

Well, I've messed this up royally, Emma told herself. "Mother, I'm sorry, I didn't call to fight with you."

"Well, you could have fooled me," Kat said coolly.

"I called to tell you some wonderful news," Emma continued, ignoring her mother's jibe. She took a deep breath and screwed her eyes closed tight. "The thing is . . ." She opened her eyes and looked at Sam and Carrie. They nodded at her encouragingly. "Well . . ." She couldn't make herself say the words. Finally, she forced herself to say the whole thing in a rush: "Kurt-asked-me-to-marry-him-and-I-said-yes."

Silence.

"You *what?*" Kat asked.

"I said," Emma repeated, forcing herself to speak more slowly, "Kurt asked me to marry him and I said yes."

"You said yes," Kat echoed.

"Yes."

"To the taxi driver," Kat added.

"He's not a taxi driver—"

"The boy does drive a taxi, does he not?" Kat asked in a frigid voice.

"Well, yes," Emma admitted, "but that's just one of the jobs that helps put him through col-lege—"

"If the boy drives a taxi, then he is a taxi driver," Kat concluded. "You have called to tell me you are marrying a taxi driver."

"You can be as nasty as you want," Emma said, "but I love Kurt and I'm going to marry him."

Silence.

"Mother? Are you there?"

"Emma, this is absolutely out of the question," Kat finally said.

"Look, I didn't call to ask your permission," Emma snapped. "I called to tell you, and to invite you to my wedding."

"Oh, and when is this lavish event to take place?" Kat inquired.

"In two weeks," Emma replied.

"Oh, my God, you're pregnant!" Kat cried.

"No, I am not pregnant!" Emma shouted. She forced herself to take a deep breath. "I am not pregnant," she repeated in a controlled voice. "I am in love. I am happy. And I hope you can be happy for me."

"But Emma," Kat protested, "I am much too young to have a married daughter. I can not possibly be one of those middle aged mother-of-the-brides!"

"Well, that's what you are, so get over it!" Emma yelled, losing all her self-control.

"There is no need for you to raise you voice," Kat said in her usual well-modulated tones. "Honestly, Emma, I raised you better than that."

You didn't raise me at all, Emma thought bitterly. *I was raised by housekeepers and nannies and teachers at Swiss boarding schools.* But she didn't say that. She didn't say anything.

"Emma, if you are not pregnant, why in God's name would you want to be married in two weeks?" Kat asked.

"Because I want to do it before Dad goes in for his heart surgery," Emma explained. "I want to make sure he can walk me down the aisle."

"That makes sense, actually," Kat said, much to Emma's surprise.

"It does?" Emma said, taken aback that her mother had agreed with her.

"Yes, it does. It's very considerate," Kat said. "But then you always were more considerate of your father's feelings than you were of mine."

I knew it wouldn't last, Emma thought. She pinched the bridge of her nose and tried to will away the awful headache that talking with her mother had brought on. "I haven't told Dad about this yet," Emma said. "I tried to reach him in Florida, but I got his machine."

"Well, you can tell him right now," Kat said. "Maybe he can talk you out of the whole thing."

"I can tell him right now?" Emma asked, bewildered.

"Yes," Kat replied. "He's downstairs in the study."

"Daddy's with you?"

"I believe I just said that," Kat confirmed regally. "Let me buzz him on the other line."

Daddy is home with Mother, Emma told herself with amazement. *Does that mean they really are getting back together? Do I want them to?*

"Brent, darling, pick up my line," Emma heard her mother say into the inter-house intercom system.

Emma heard a click.

"Yes?" her father said.

"It's me, Dad."

"Sweetheart!" Brent Cresswell's voice boomed through the phone. "How good to hear from you!"

Emma smiled. Not long ago, her father's voice had been a thin rasp, as he lay in a hospital bed recovering from a massive heart attack. *It's so good to hear him sound just like his old self*, Emma thought.

"Emma has news," Kat said.

"Do you, honey?" her father asked.

"Yes," Emma replied. "I'm . . . I'm getting married."

Silence.

"Married?" Brent Cresswell asked.

"Yes," Emma insisted for what she felt was the five thousandth time. "Kurt asked me and I said yes."

"Well, I'm surprised," her father said slowly. "You're kind of young . . ."

"I know, Daddy," Emma said. "But I really love Kurt. You met him. You know how great he is."

"He is a very nice young man, but—"

"And after your heart attack, you're the one who told me I had to follow my own heart and not do what you wanted me to do or what Mother wanted me to do," Emma continued earnestly. "Well, this is really, truly what I want. And I want you to be happy for me."

Silence.

"Emma, sweetheart, you're right," her father said.

"I am?"

"Absolutely," Brent Cresswell said. "If you're happy, I'm happy."

"Brent!" Kat cried into the phone.

"Kat, she's right," he told his ex-wife. "Now, when's the wedding?"

"Two weeks from Sunday," Emma told her father with tears in her eyes.

"So soon?" he asked.

"So you can walk me down the aisle, Daddy," she said softly.

"Emma . . ." her father said, gruffness masking the tears in his voice. "And I will. I'll be the proudest man on earth."

"Well, I think the two of you have lost your senses!" Kat exclaimed.

I'm going to do the mature thing, Emma told herself firmly. "Mother, will you walk me down the aisle with Daddy?"

"We were supposed to be on our cruise that Sunday," Kat reminded her ex-husband petulantly.

"Kat, there are lots of cruises," Brent said gently.

Silence.

"Oh, all right," Kat finally agreed. "But I don't know how you expect me to have a dress made in two weeks!"

"Oh, I'm sure you'll manage," Brent said smoothly.

"I'll call you both soon and give you more details," Emma told her parents. "Uh, Daddy, should I reach you at this number?"

"You just did," he replied, a laugh in his voice.

"Does that mean the two of you—?" Emma asked.

"Please, Emma," Kat said frostily. "The personal lives of your parents are really none of your business."

Emma couldn't decide if that was true or not, but she decided to quit while she actually had something like agreement going on between the three of them. She said her good-byes and hung up.

"Well?" Sam asked expectantly.

"My dad was there," Emma said.

"That much we gathered," Sam replied. "Give us the dirt."

"The dirt," Emma said slowly, "is that my father and my mother have both agreed to walk me down the aisle. Together."

Carrie gave Emma a hug. "I'm so happy for you."

"I'm in a state of shock," Emma said. Then slowly a smile spread across her face. "They actually, really, truly agreed! I told them, and they agreed!"

"This should be on the front page of the *Breakers!*" Sam exclaimed. "Kat Cresswell Admits to Having Daughter Old Enough to Wed!'"

"You guys," Emma whispered, her eyes shining, "I can't believe it—I'm getting married!"

SEVEN

"I'm the happiest guy on the planet," Kurt said, holding Emma even closer to him. They sat together in the brisk night air at the end of the main pier. There was some sort of nighttime powerboat regatta underway, and in the distance, red and white lights from the vessels skittered to and fro on the ocean like giant-sized water beetles.

"Ditto," Emma murmured, sliding herself even deeper into Kurt's strong arms.

"Gee, you don't look a thing like a guy," he teased.

"Really? What was your first clue?"

"The way you look," Kurt answered solemnly. "No, the way you smell." He nuzzled into her neck and sniffed deeply. "No, no, it's the way you feel." He ran his hand down to the lower curve of her back.

Emma laughed. "I think it must be illegal to be this happy!"

"So," Kurt whispered, "when you were a little girl, what was your dream wedding?"

This is too much bliss for me, Emma thought to herself. *When is it going to stop? He wants me to describe my dream wedding to him, so I can have exactly what I always dreamed.*

"Probably the same dream every girl has," Emma murmured, feeling the cool night breeze ruffle her hair. She pulled the pink embroidered jean jacket she was wearing more closely around her.

"What's that?"

"You know, a white dress with a train—" Emma whispered.

"Done," Kurt said emphatically.

Emma reached over and kissed him on the lips gently.

"Go on," Kurt insisted. "I like how we're keeping score."

"My best friends as bridesmaids—" she continued.

"Done," Kurt stated.

Emma kissed him again.

"I'm rolling here," Kurt joked. "Don't stop now."

"I won't," Emma replied. She kissed him again.

"What else?" Kurt asked.

"A beautiful setting," she mused.

"Absolutely," Kurt responded. "Anything else?"

Emma smiled and tried to think all the way back to her childhood, to the dream wedding she'd always had in her mind, which was just like the many weddings of royalty and the rich and famous that she had attended with her parents.

"Oh, I don't know," Emma said dreamily.

"No other ideas?" Kurt asked. "You've got to give me something else to agree to here. My lips are getting lonesome."

"Shouldn't happen," Emma answered, as she reached over to kiss Kurt one more time.

"So?" Kurt asked playfully.

"I guess," Emma said slowly, "just the biggest, most romantic, most lavish, most incredible wedding and party ever. Elegant. Yes, that's it, elegant!"

Emma felt Kurt stiffen somewhat next to her.

"You okay?" she asked.

"Fine," he said tersely.

"You aren't going to say 'done'?" she queried.

"No," Kurt replied evenly. "I'm not going to say done because our wedding isn't going to be that way."

She looked at him. "You're kidding."

"No, I'm serious," Kurt said.

"But—"

"Think about it, Em," Kurt interrupted, "how comfortable would my family be at a wedding that looks like something you'd see on *Lifestyles of the Rich and Famous*?"

Emma almost asked him how comfortable her family would be at a wedding held at Rubie's restaurant, where the main course would be fried codfish, but she held her tongue.

"I mean it," Kurt went on, gently but emphatically. "I think—"

"Are you worried about the money?" Emma asked, getting a sudden flash of intuition.

"It's not that," Kurt replied, "it's just that—"

"It is that," Emma countered. "Kurt, we should enjoy the fact that we can afford any kind of a wedding we want. We're so lucky."

"*We're* not lucky," Kurt said pointedly, "*you're* lucky."

I can't believe I'm hearing this, Emma said to herself. *He's holding out because he's too proud to have a big wedding. This is ridiculous!*

"Kurt," she said patiently, "if you were rich and I was . . . I mean, if I didn't have much money, you would tell me that everything you had was mine, wouldn't you?"

"That's different," Kurt insisted.

"Why?" Emma asked. "Because you're a guy? That's ridiculous!"

"It's not ridiculous," Kurt countered stubbornly. "I plan to earn every penny I ever have in this world, and that's that."

God, I bet that's exactly how my father felt

when he married my mother, Emma thought. *Daddy was poor, and mother was so rich, and he ended up spending all of his time making his own fortune just to prove to the world that he didn't marry her for her money. He was so busy making his fortune that he neglected his family, and he and my mother ended up divorced . . .*

Kurt pulled Emma closer. "I don't want to fight about this, babe," he said softly.

"Me, either," she agreed fervently. "But, well, usually the bride gets to decide the kind of wedding she wants. I mean, it's customary for the bride's family to pay for the wedding and all."

"Meaning that I can't afford a wedding?" Kurt asked.

"No!" Emma cried. "Don't get so touchy! I just meant that I'm only planning on getting married once in my life, and I really, really want it to be the way I always dreamed it would be!"

"Hey," Kurt exclaimed, "don't I get a say in this?"

Emma stopped herself. *He's right,* she thought. *I'm not being fair. I should at least give him the opportunity to tell me what he has in mind. A marriage is a partnership, right?*

"Of course you do," Emma agreed. "We should decide the whole thing together. "Tell me what you'd like."

"Well," Kurt began, "I was thinking of a small wedding—just our parents, brothers and sisters, closest friends—outside, on the dunes, at sunset."

Emma groaned inwardly. "And what would we do afterwards," she said sweetly, "get Rubie to put on a fish fry for us?"

"You know," Kurt mused, "that's not a bad idea."

Emma took a deep breath and tried to calm herself. This was not going well at all.

"Kurt," she said finally, "that's a lovely idea for a wedding. But it's not going to be our wedding."

"Says who?" Kurt asked pointedly.

"Me," Emma replied. "I did not grow up to have a wedding that I'm going to be embarrassed about."

"If you'd be embarrassed about a wedding like that," Kurt said hotly, "you'd be embarrassed about marrying me!"

"No!" Emma cried, "that's not what I meant."

Kurt leaped to his feet. "So what did you mean, exactly?"

Emma scrambled up next to him. "Kurt, please, it isn't like that—"

"What, did you think that just because you have the bucks you get to call the shots?" Kurt challenged.

"No, I thought because I'm the bride I get to call the shots!" she shouted.

"You can really be a spoiled brat sometimes,

Emma," Kurt said in a steely voice. "You're just used to getting your own way."

"That's not true!"

"It is true," Kurt insisted. "You could show a little sensitivity about how my family might feel instead of just thinking about yourself all the time!"

"Argghhh!" Emma screamed with frustration. "You are being completely unreasonable!"

"Yeah," Kurt said. "I'm unreasonable and I'm poor and I'm proud. That's who the hell I am. So you better just think things over, Em. Because you're going to be stuck with me as your husband for the rest of your life!"

Kurt stomped off into the night, leaving Emma on the end of the pier in tears, all alone.

"So he called you later and apologized?" Carrie said to Emma, as they sat together with Sam in the waiting room of Coastal Party Service, a catering firm in Portland. It was the next morning, and Emma had made arrangements for her, Carrie, and Sam to come in and audition singers for the wedding.

"Yes," said Emma, who had just told them the story of her fight with Kurt the night before. "Most of it was just pre-wedding jitters, I think. It was such a silly fight!"

"Fight number one," Sam pronounced breezily. "You've got a few more coming to you."

"Why do you say that?" Emma asked. "I love him."

"You're going to be married," Sam stated, as if that answered the question.

"Anyway," Emma said, ignoring Sam, "he told me that he was sorry that he overreacted, and that any kind of wedding I wanted would be okay with him."

"See, that's one of the great things about Kurt," Carrie said warmly. "He's the kind of guy who can admit to his mistakes."

"As long as he knows that asking me to marry him wasn't one of them," Emma added with a small smile.

"Hey, did you remember to call the Sunset Inn this morning to book the ballroom?" Sam asked Emma.

"Yes, I did and yes, it's free," Emma said. "We really lucked out. It had been booked months ago for a party, but the people called a few days ago and cancelled."

"You lead a charmed life," Carrie told Emma.

"Miss Cresswell?" A pudgy, middle-aged man came into the reception area.

"That's me," Emma said, standing up.

"Hi there, I'm Bill Coastal," he shook her hand. "I run this place. We're ready with your singers. I got in a couple. You didn't give me much notice. If you don't like what you see, I can give you tapes of a few more."

"That would be fine," Emma said.

"Also, I hope you understand that each of these singers sings with a band, but there was no way could I get the entire band in here on this kind of notice. Usually the girls go to hear them at a gig, you know?"

Emma nodded.

"So, at least you can hear the singers. You'll have to kind of use your imagination for the rest."

Mr. Coastal ushered the three girls into a tiny room, where there was a karoake machine that played the instrumental tracks to popular songs and an even tinier stage.

The first singer walked in—a voluptuous redhead with more freckles than Sam had and about thirty-five years old.

"Hi, I'm Margaret Sheehan," she told the girls. She pressed some buttons on the control box and picked up the mike. A video and an instrumental track to Billy Joel's "I Love You Just the Way You Are" began. Margaret had a tiny, thin voice that had a tenuous grasp on the melody.

"Thanks, that's fine," Emma assured her quickly before she could punch in a second tune.

"I could do an up-tempo," Margaret said. "I was kind of nervous just now—"

"Th-thank you," Emma stammered, as she and her friends tried to keep their cool. "Thank you very much."

Margaret Sheehan exited, looking chagrined.

The next person to audition was a striking-looking black girl in her twenties, who came in wearing a black catsuit topped by a cropped red jacket with black braiding. He name was Tawana Singleton, and she gave an absolutely great audition. She sang an up-tempo, a ballad, and then belted out "Amazing Grace" a capella. When she was done, the girls burst into wild applause.

"You're hired!" Emma cried, so happy that she had found the singer she was looking for so quickly. "What band do you sing with?"

"Sweetsounds," Tawana replied. "They're great."

"Well, if they're half as terrific as you are, they must be incredible," Carrie told her.

"Thanks," Tawana answered with a grin.

"What do you charge?" Carrie asked, pulling out a notebook that had "EMMA'S WEDDING" written in big block letters on the front of it.

"What difference does it make?" Sam hissed. "Emma can afford it."

"What Sam really means," Carrie hastened to explain, lest Tawana get the impression that she could raise her price to the roof, "is that Emma really cares about great music. Right, Emma?"

"Right!" Emma seconded.

"With my band, we'll be twelve hundred dollars for the night," Tawana said breezily. "We can do all that traditional wedding stuff, introduce you, the whole garter thing, the intros, the cake-cutting—believe me, we've done tons of these."

"Can some of our friends come up and sing?" Sam asked pointedly. "The bride and I are in Flirting With Danger."

"Is that right?" Tawana said. "I know that band. I've always wanted to meet that lead singer—what's his name?"

"Billy Sampson, and he's her boyfriend," Sam said, jerking her head toward Carrie.

Tawana laughed. "I said I wanted to meet him, not jump him! I think he's a terrific singer."

"Well, he'll be at the wedding," Emma assured her.

"He can certainly sing," Tawana said. "It's your wedding—you can have anyone sing you want!"

"So it's settled," Carrie stated, fetching a pen from her purse. "You're hired. It's at the Sunset Inn on the island."

"Cool," Tawana said. "I'll just need a deposit check for half the amount, and I'll see you two weeks from Saturday night."

"You mean Sunday," Carrie corrected her.

"Bill Coastal told me Saturday. I can't do Sunday," Tawana responded, opening her Filofax and checking the date. "That's right. I'm singing the national anthem at Fenway Park, then doing a party in Boston. Sorry."

Emma, Carrie, and Sam looked at one another and let out a collective groan.

"You're sure about this?" Sam asked her. "There's going to be some very important people at the wedding."

"Hon, the party in Boston is for the Kennedys," Tawana said smoothly. "I'm so sorry. Go bitch at Bill. Anyway, nice to have met you."

Tawana breezed out of the room. The girls sat there, dumbfounded.

Bill Coastal stuck his head in.

"There was one other girl, but she left," he reported.

"We loved Tawana, but you told her the wrong date," Carrie told him.

He shrugged. "Stuff happens."

"What are we going to do?" Carrie asked no one in particular.

"Beats me," Sam answered.

Just then the phone rang right outside the tiny room.

"Excuse me," Coastal said, and went to get it. A moment later, he popped his head back in the room.

"For you," he said to Emma.

"Me?" Emma asked, surprised. Coastal nodded and handed the phone to her.

"Emma Cresswell speaking," Emma said.

A somewhat shaky young male voice spoke up. "Hi, Emma," it said, "it's Ian Templeton."

Emma put her hand over the receiver for a

moment. "It's Ian Templeton," she hissed to her friends.

Carrie and Sam both shrugged, wondering why Ian was calling.

"Hi, Ian," Emma said, "how do you happen to be calling me here?"

"Oh, Carrie told me where you were going," Ian said nervously.

"I see," Emma replied, even though she didn't have a clue. "What can I do for you?"

"Well," Ian responded, "I understand that you might be looking for a band for your wedding."

"Yessss," Emma said slowly.

"Well," Ian said hesitantly, "I just wanted you to know that my band, Lord Whitehead and the Zit People, is available."

"I see," Emma said gravely, practically choking on her response. "Could you hold on just a moment?"

Emma covered the receiver again. "He wants the Zits to play the wedding!"

"Incredible!" Carrie grinned.

"Unbelievable," Emma agreed.

"Why not?" Sam offered.

"Sam!" Emma and Carrie scolded at once.

Emma turned back to the phone.

"Well, Ian, thank you for the offer," Emma managed.

"All we're asking for is a chance to show you what we can do!" Ian said emphatically. "All we're asking for is a chance! Give us a chance."

Okay, I have to tell him no, Emma thought to herself. *But be nice!*

"Look Ian," Emma said softly, "I really appreciate your having called me, but . . . we just hired a band."

"You did?" Ian said, sounding crestfallen.

"Right," Emma said. "We've . . . uh, already given them a deposit check and everything."

"You mean I'm too late?" Ian asked.

"Sorry," Emma told him.

Ian sighed heavily into the phone. "Well, just let me ask you this. If I had called earlier, before you hired a band, would you have considered the Zits?"

It's only a little white lie, Emma told herself.

"Yes, I would have considered the Zits," Emma told him.

"Thanks," Ian said. "Well, maybe your next wedding. Bye!"

A few hours after Emma and her friends got back to the island from the fruitless auditions, Emma was in the living room of the Hewitts', flipping through a *Brides* magazine, when the phone rang.

"Hewitt residence, Emma Cresswell speaking," Emma said automatically.

"Hello, darling!" a gay voice cried. "It's your mother!"

Great. Just who I wanted to talk to, Emma thought.

"Hello, Mother," Emma said, trying to muster a little enthusiasm.

"Really, Emma," Kat said, "you should be more excited. You're getting married in two weeks!"

"Sorry, Mother," Emma replied, "it's just that there's so much to do."

"Exactly," Kat replied.

"Exactly what?"

"Exactly why I want to introduce you to someone," Kat answered. "Lord Owen, are you there?"

"At your service, my dear," an upper-crust British-sounding male voice responded.

"Emma, introduce yourself to Lord Owen Witherspoon," Kat ordered.

"Hello," Emma responded automatically, completely clueless.

"Emma, Lord Owen is the finest wedding planner in the western hemisphere," Kat explained. "We are so lucky that he is available on such short notice to do your wedding!"

"What do you mean?" Emma answered, not sure she was following the conversation.

"Lord Owen will arrive tomorrow morning at nine; you're to pick him up at the ferryport," Kat commanded.

"But—"

"But nothing, Emma," Kat said in her most businesslike voice. "There's two weeks to get ready; we don't have a moment to lose."

"But—" Emma began.

"Miss Cresswell, if we might interrupt?" Lord Owen asked smoothly.

"What?" Emma said with irritation.

"Normally we are booked one to two years in advance of an event," Lord Owen explained haughtily.

"Well, no need to make an exception for me," Emma told him dryly.

"Quite right," Lord Owen agreed. "And yet how could we possibly allow Katerina Cresswell's daughter to be married without our assistance?"

"Excuse me," Emma said, "I don't want to be rude, but I really don't need any help—"

"How droll," Lord Owen interrupted again. "Did we plan on an event on the beach with flowers in our hair and our friends in tie dye?"

"No, we planned on an event that we can plan with our friends," Emma replied frostily.

"Um-hummmm," Lord Owen replied. "And how far have we gotten?"

"Not very," Emma admitted with a sigh.

"Goody," Lord Owen replied in a flat voice. "Think how much less we'll need to undo."

"Emma, please," Kat said. "You cannot plan a wedding by yourself in two weeks! I'm trying to help you!"

I suppose she's right, Emma decided. *I couldn't*

even find a band this morning. "You won't try to tell me what to do, will you?" Emma asked.

"We live to serve," Lord Owen said in withering tones. "Now, what is the groom's name?"

"Kurt," Emma answered.

"Kurt," Lord Owen repeated. "Which is short for . . . ?"

"Short for nothing," Emma said. "Just Kurt."

"Plebian," Lord Owen commented dryly. "Oh, well, we will consider it the challenge of our career. Tomorrow morning, then—we can barely contain our excitement."

Emma said good-bye and hung up the phone, shaking her head.

Just what I need, she thought. *Lord Owen Witherspoon coordinating my wedding. At my mother's expense. Because she's afraid my wedding will be a disaster otherwise.*

Emma was afraid to admit it, but for once her mother could be right.

EIGHT

"I still don't see why we need this guy," Kurt groused.

It was the next morning, and he and Emma were waiting for Lord Owen's ferry at the ferryport. Emma had called Kurt the night before, and he had agreed to come with her to meet the wedding consultant.

"I already explained it to you," Emma said patiently. "It's just impossible for me to plan all of this in two weeks. For once I actually have to agree with my mother."

"Well, okay," Kurt agreed. "As long as this guy doesn't try to dictate to us what we should have or do."

"Oh, I'm sure he won't," Emma assured Kurt. *I only hope I'm right,* she added to herself with trepidation. "Let's get out of the car and wait at the dock," she suggested.

They walked leisurely over to the dock and leaned against a wooden piling. The morning sun warmed Emma's face. "Mmmmm, that feels great," she said, closing her eyes and lifting her chin to the sky.

"Do you know how beautiful you look?" Kurt asked her.

"I think it must be my outfit," Emma teased. She was wearing jeans, a plain white man's T-shirt, and white Nikes.

Kurt leaned over and kissed her softly. "You are going to be some gorgeous bride."

Emma opened her eyes and smiled at Kurt. "Every bride looks beautiful," she said. She put her arms around his neck. "I love you so much," she whispered.

"Mrs. Ackerman," Kurt said out loud, trying out the sound of it. "Wow."

Something funny hit Emma in the pit of her stomach. "That doesn't sound like it could be me," she said. "It sounds like someone's mother. Yours!"

"Well, it will be you soon," Kurt pointed out. "Like it?"

"What if ... what if I didn't want to change my name?" Emma asked slowly.

Kurt stared at her. "Is that what you want?"

"I don't know," Emma admitted. "I guess I never really thought about it before. But now that I hear you say it, it seems ... odd to be Mrs. someone-else."

"Well, it's pretty traditional," Kurt said. "It's so much easier on the kids when Mom and Dad have the same last name."

"That's true, I guess," Emma agreed. "But kids! Now, that is something in the really distant future!"

"That we agree on," Kurt said with a laugh, kissing Emma again. "Although personally I think practicing to make them is going to be excellent."

Emma laughed. "Me, too," she agreed. "I'll just have to think about the name thing, okay?" Emma said.

"Okay," Kurt agreed.

Emma Ackerman, she thought to herself. *Could I really be Emma Ackerman? But I like being Emma Cresswell! On the other hand, what kind of way is it to start a marriage if I don't even want to share his name? This is one I'm going to have to think over very seriously.*

She noticed the ferry pulling closer to the dock. "Here he comes!" she said, cocking her head toward the boat.

Emma and Kurt watched the ferry pull into port and begin to disgorge the passengers. Finally a tall, elegantly dressed man in an impeccable suit, his silver hair perfectly groomed, walked down the gangplank. He pulled a pair of designer sunglasses out of his pocket and put them on, then looked around the dock.

"I bet that's him," Emma said. "Come on." Emma and Kurt walked hand-in-hand over to the gentleman. "Excuse me, are you Lord Owen?"

"I am," the man said. He raised his sunglasses and peered at her from underneath them. "Miss Cresswell, we presume?"

"Please call me Emma," Emma said. "And this is my fiancé, Kurt Ackerman. Kurt, this is Lord Owen Witherspoon."

"Call me Kurt," Kurt said in a friendly voice, and shook the older gentleman's hand.

"Call me Lord Owen," the older man instructed them. He set his sunglasses back on his nose.

"Is this your only bag?" Kurt asked, lifting the small carryon Lord Owen had set down beside him.

"Dear boy, we are going to be here for two weeks," Lord Owen said. "We came prepared."

"Where the hell is he?" a young ferryhand was yelling as he struggled down the gangplank with four huge designer suitcases. He caught sight of Lord Owen and struggled toward him with the luggage.

"Very good," Lord Owen said. He turned to Emma. "The transportation—?"

"Oh, I have my employer's car," Emma explained, and led the way to the Mercedes. Kurt picked up two of the bags and then caught Emma's eye with a look that said "can-you-believe-this-guy?"

"Right this way," Emma said, trying to ignore Kurt's looks and the ferryhand's grumbling under his breath.

"Thank you so much," Lord Owen told the young man. The ferryhand dropped the luggage and stood there. Lord Owen turned and stared pointedly at Emma.

"Oh, just a minute!" Emma cried, blushing with the realization that the guy was waiting for a tip. She pulled a few bills out of her purse. "Thank you," she said, handing him the money.

"Anytime," the ferryhand said cheerfully when he saw the size of his tip. He touched his cap and walked away.

"If you like, we can keep a running charge of these piddling items and bill you," Lord Owen said as Emma unlocked the trunk of the car.

"Yes, that would be easier," Emma agreed.

Kurt put the luggage in the trunk and they all got in the car. Lord Owen got in front next to Emma, which left Kurt to sit in the back seat by himself.

"Well, we certainly have our work cut out for us, don't we," Lord Owen said. He opened a small leather notebook and pulled a silver pen from his pocket. "Time and place is set, is it not?"

"It is," Emma said, as she pulled the car out of the ferry parking lot. "We'll be in the main ballroom of the Sunset Inn—it's lovely."

"I'm sure we'll cluck with joy when we see it," Lord Owen avowed. "So, today we need to discuss invitations, colors, dining arrangements, menu, music, flowers, dress of the wedding party—and that is only the beginning."

Emma felt dizzy. "It seems overwhelming."

"Of course," Lord Owen agreed. "That is why we are here."

"Excuse me," Kurt said irritably from the back seat, "but who is this 'we' you keep referring to? I mean, as far as I can see, you're the only one here."

Lord Owen turned around and lifted his sunglasses to regard Kurt as if he were viewing a particularly loathsome insect under a microscope. "Are we feeling a wee bit testy?"

"No, we are not," Kurt snapped.

"Perhaps we need a little nap," Lord Owen suggested, and turned back around in his seat.

Emma winced. "Would you like me drop you at the country club, sweetie?" she asked Kurt.

"The sooner the better," he mumbled, slumping down in the back seat.

Through her rearview mirror Emma could see that he had murder in his eyes. Well, I'll have to get Lord Owen alone and set him straight on treating Kurt with more respect, Emma thought. Otherwise this is going to be a total disaster!

"We're supposed to turn left on Fairfax Street," Sam read from her directions. "It should be a light."

It was three hours later, and the girls were on their way to the Bridal Shoppe in Portland to look at bridesmaids dresses and wedding gowns.

"From what you've been telling us about Lord Owen, I'm surprised he's letting us go off on our own to look at dresses," Carrie said from the back seat of the car.

"Actually, he doesn't know," Emma confessed. "He told me—"

"Hey, this is Fairfax coming up," Sam interrupted.

"Thanks," Emma said, getting into the left turn lane. "Anyway, I spent all morning with him at the Sunset Inn going over all these details—he's already driving me crazy and Kurt is going to have a fit—and then I told him I had to work for a few hours and I slipped out and came to pick the two of you up."

"Wouldn't you think he'd insist on coming with us?" Carrie asked.

"No," Emma replied, "I think he'd faint dead away if I told him I planned to try to find a gown off the rack. How far are we supposed to go on this street, Sam?"

"Two miles," Sam replied. "It'll be a large white building on the right."

"How could you possibly get a gown designed and made in two weeks?" Carrie queried.

"Believe me, my mother has connections," Emma said. "Little fingers would sew seed pearls day and night, and I'd have the gown of my mother's dreams."

"So, what's the gown of *your* dreams?" Carrie wondered.

"I don't know," Emma admitted. "But I'll know it when I see it."

"Well, somehow I don't see Emma Cresswell in an off-the-rack number from the Bridal Shoppe," Sam said. "I will be mega-shocked if we find you a dress there."

"Oh, there it is," Carrie said, pointing to a large building on the right. "It looks like there's a parking lot in back."

Emma turned right and found a parking space, and the girls walked into the building. A bell tinkled when they entered the front door.

"What first?" Carrie asked. "Bridal or bridesmaids?"

"Bridal, of course," Sam answered for Emma. "This is one time when I bow to Emma."

"Thanks," Emma said cheerfully.

A cherubic-looking middle-aged woman in a lime-green suit with a lime-green and white frilly polka-dot blouse and lime-green high heels came over to the girls. "Hello, girls, my name is Mrs. Fletcher. May I help you?"

"Yes," Emma said. "I'm getting married and these are my bridesmaids. We'd like to look at bridal gowns and bridesmaids dresses."

"Lovely! I just love weddings, don't you?" the woman asked enthusiastically.

"Especially mine!" Emma said with a laugh.

Mrs. Fletcher laughed heartily. "Aren't you sweet, dear! I'll be just so happy to help you. Tell me something about the type of gown your looking for—we have hundreds—it will help me narrow it down for you."

"I don't actually know," Emma said.

"Oh, that's all right," Mrs. Fletcher assured Emma cheerfully, "a lot of girls don't know when they walk in the door. Well, shall we discuss price range? Perhaps that will help. Our gowns range from three hundred dollars to five thousand dollars."

"Price is no object," Emma said easily.

"I see," Mrs. Fletcher said smoothly after a beat of silence. "Well! How nice for you! Why don't I just take you girls back to the gown room and let you peruse."

"Wonderful," Emma agreed.

"You're about a size five?" Mrs. Fletcher asked Emma.

"Right," Emma replied.

Mrs. Fletcher led them through the first room, which was filled with bridesmaids' dresses, and through a rear door into a huge, cavernous room filled with rack after rack of wedding gowns. "Here we are. We have the largest selection of wedding gowns in New England," Mrs. Fletcher said proudly.

"That's what *Brides* magazine said," Emma murmured, looking around her at the endless rows of white gowns.

"See what you like, and call me if you need anything, dear," Mrs. Fletcher said, and walked away.

"I suggest we don't solicit her opinion," Sam whispered. "That lime-green number she's wearing is the ugliest outfit I've ever seen."

"Oh, too bad," Emma moaned, "I just picked lime-green as one of the colors for the wedding!"

"I know you're kidding," Sam replied.

"But you'd look so fetching in a lime-green gown," Emma said. "With some tasteful pumps dyed to match?"

"A real fashion police special," Sam said.

"God, where do we even begin?" Carrie asked, pulling out a gown and then dropping it back into the rack.

"At the beginning, I guess," Emma said. "How about if we each pick a rack, and if anyone finds anything good we show the others."

"But what if we don't like what you like?" Carrie asked.

"Carrie, you two know me better than anyone in the world," Emma said. "You guys know what I like."

"Well, we know you like white," Sam pointed out, pawing through her rack, "which seems to come in handy in a wedding gown."

"How about this?" Carrie asked, holding out an empire-waist gown with a sweetheart neckline and lots of lace.

"Too . . . something," Emma said, making a face.

Carrie shrugged and put the gown back.

The three looked in silence for a few minutes.

"Hey, how about this?" Sam asked, holding out a gown with a halter neckline and a very tight-fitted skirt with a slit all the way up one leg. "Mondo sexy!"

"Sam, you would wear that, not me," Emma pointed out.

"You're right," Sam said, looking at the gown. "I'd look fabulous in this."

They went through rack after rack of wedding dresses, but every dress that either Carrie or Sam suggested Emma didn't like.

"This isn't getting us anywhere," Carrie said after about an hour of fruitless searching. "And the dresses are all starting to sort of blur together in my mind."

"How about the world's first nude wedding?" Sam suggested. "It'll be so easy to color coordinate."

"Well, girls, how's it going?" Mrs. Fletcher asked, walking briskly into the room.

"Not very well," Emma admitted. "I don't seem to find anything that really speaks to me."

"Well, perhaps a break from white, white, white will help," Mrs. Fletcher said.

"But I want a white wedding gown," Emma protested.

"No," Mrs. Fletcher laughed. "I meant, why not look for bridesmaids dresses for a while and then come back to this?"

"Oh. Good idea," Emma agreed.

"Fine, then follow me!"

They went back into the front room, where the dresses looked particularly colorful in contrast to all the white wedding gowns.

"So, what are your colors?" Mrs. Fletcher asked.

Emma had spent endless time on just this subject with Lord Owen. He had suggested graduated shades of eggshell, cream, wheat, and beige—he insisted that a sort of atonal-colored wedding was all the rage in Europe. *I told him I didn't care, that I wasn't in Europe and I wanted some color*, Emma remembered. *Of course, I never did decide what color.*

"My colors . . ." Emma said slowly.

Carrie and Sam looked at her expectantly.

Why is this so incredibly difficult for me to decide? Emma asked herself. *Okay. I'm just going to pick. Right now.* She closed her eyes and pictured the beach at Sunset Island, and in her mind's eye she saw the delicate color of the inside of a seashell.

"Pale pink," she finally said. "Pale pink and white."

"Oh, Emma," Carrie laughed, "that is so *you!*"

"You're sure you don't want anything a bit more striking?" Mrs. Fletcher asked. "My daughter got married last year. Her colors were lime-green and kelly-green."

"No!" Sam cried, feigning surprise.

"Honestly!" Mrs. Fletcher assured her. "It was bold, but fabulous! And there's a new designer from New Jersey making the most gorgeous lime-green gowns in polyester this season. They truly do not wrinkle!"

"It's sounds . . . unique," Emma said, "but I'm not much of a lime girl."

"Oh, well, fine," Mrs. Fletcher said with a cheerful shrug. "let's just go over to the pale pink gowns." They walked across the room to a long rack with gowns of every shade of pink imaginable. "Here you are. Take all the time you need. The dressing rooms are right behind you."

"Thank you," Emma told her.

"Emma, you know I love you like a sister," Sam said, pushing through the gowns, "but I will look horrid in baby pink and you should be shot for forcing it on me."

"You'll look fine," Carrie told her. "Let's find a style we all like."

"Short or long?" Sam asked Emma.

"You guys can pick," Emma said.

"How about this?" Sam asked. It was a pale pink strapless lace sheath slit up one leg.

"Sam, I will look like a whale in that," Carrie said. "I couldn't fit one hip into that dress."

Sam reluctantly put it back on the rack.

"God, most of these are horrendous," Carrie said. "They look like someone went bow crazy and just stuck them on everything. Look at this one! It's got a huge bow right over the butt! Just what I need! I might as well wear a neon sign that reads: HERE LIES TEN EXTRA POUNDS!"

"Carrie, you are one hot mama," said Sam. "I may be the tall, thin, wild type, but you know that I would kill for a set of lungs like yours!"

"Hey, how about this?" Emma asked. She held up a sleeveless pink chiffon dress with a low rounded neckline, a fitted cummerbund waist, and a full, flowing chiffon skirt in various shades of pink that came to just above the knees.

"Woah, baby, very Marilyn Monroe!" Sam hooted.

"I love it," Carrie said. "Frankly, I'm surprised something that tasteful found its way into this store," she added in a whisper.

"Let's find our sizes and try them on," Sam said. "Here's a six for me and a ten for you." She handed Carrie a dress.

"In my next life, I'm coming back as someone who wears a dress size with one number in it," Carrie said with a sigh as they carried their dresses back into the dressing room.

Both girls quickly tried on the dresses and came back out.

"Wow, you look fabulous!" Emma cried. "I love them!"

Carrie and Sam whirled around in front of a three-way mirror. The swirly chiffon of their skirts whirled out around their legs.

"It's really a pretty dress," Carrie said.

"Yeah, I am such a babe!" Sam shrieked with happiness. She looked down at the neckline of the dress. "Now if only you would loan me your hooters, I would be walking perfection."

"Sorry, they're not detachable," Carrie said dryly.

"You both look great," Emma said. "I think this is really it!"

Sam reached for the ticket and looked at the price. "Yowza! The price on this puppy is five hundred dollars! No way can I afford that!"

"Well, who said anything about you paying for it?" Emma asked.

"I thought bridesmaids always paid for their own dresses," Sam said with a self-conscious shrug.

"Sam, consider it a gift from Kat Cresswell," Emma said, "who will never even know she spent the money."

"You're sure?" Carrie asked. "Because we can look for something less expensive—"

"I'm positive!" Emma said firmly. "Let's just be happy that we actually found you guys dresses!"

"Why, you girls have found our newest bridesmaid dress!" Mrs. Fletcher cried when she saw the girls. "And you look lovely in it!"

"Thanks," Carrie said, going back into the dressing room.

"We'll take both of those," Emma told the saleswoman.

"Fine, dear," Mrs. Fletcher said. "And now we return to your search for a gown, right?"

"I think I've seen as many as I can look through in one day," Emma told her.

"I understand," Mrs. Fletcher said. "You just give yourself a few days off and then come back in with a fresh eye."

"That's kind of difficult," Emma said with a sigh. "You see, I'm getting married in two weeks."

"Two weeks?" Mrs. Fletcher repeated, aghast. Her eyes flew to Emma's stomach and then flitted away.

No, I'm not pregnant! Emma wanted to yell, but she was too well-bred to say anything.

Emma put the purchases on one of her credit cards, and the girls drove back to the ferry, and then rode back to the island. By the time Emma got back to the Hewitts' she was exhausted.

"Did you find a wedding gown?" Jane asked when Emma came in.

"No," Emma replied with a sigh. "I hated everything I looked at! And I keep hearing this voice in my head calling, 'Two weeks! Two weeks! You have less than two weeks!'"

"Hang in there," Jane said sympathetically.

"I'm going to go upstairs and take a shower," Emma said. "That is, if there's nothing you need me for right away."

"No, no one but me is even here at the moment," Jane said easily. "Oh, Lord Owen called. He said to call him back the instant you got in. And Kurt called and left this message, and I quote: 'That Lord Owen guy has got to go.' He wants you to call him at the club. I'm going to be in the back gardening, so could you get the phone if it rings?"

"Thanks, Jane," Emma said. She trudged upstairs and went to her room, pulled off her clothes, and stepped into a steaming hot shower. *I'm not looking forward to calling either one of them at this moment*, Emma thought. *Kurt can't stand Lord Owen—and I don't blame him—but Lord Owen knows everything about pulling a wedding together and I know nothing.*

Just as she was about to shampoo her hair, the phone rang. She jumped out of the shower, grabbed a towel, and padded to the phone dripping wet.

"Hewitt residence, Emma Cresswell speaking."

"Emma," a low male voice said into the phone.

"Kurt, listen, I know you hate Lord Owen—" Emma began.

"It's not Kurt," the deep voice said. "It's Adam Briarly."

Suddenly Emma felt like she couldn't breathe. She fell back onto the bed, ignoring the fact that

119

she was soaking wet. Adam. Sam's half-brother. The guy she had fallen head-over-heels for when she'd been in California. The guy she couldn't keep her hands off of, and he couldn't keep his hands off of her.

The guy who, just for a little while, had made her forget all about Kurt Ackerman.

NINE

"Adam," Emma said, at a total loss for words. "I can't believe it's you."

Emma's mind spun back to earlier in the summer. She saw the whole thing unfold in her mind like a movie being played back at high speed, but where she caught every single frame in her mind's eye.

She, Carrie, and Sam had gone out to California, both for the big Graham Perry/Billy Joel concert in San Francisco and to visit Sam's birth mother, Susan Briarly. They'd met Susan and her family, all right, and part of that family was Sam's half-brother, Adam.

Adam. A film student at UCLA. Unbelievably handsome, smart, intense, an artist who dreamed of becoming a film director. *The attraction between us was electric*, Emma remembered, a thrill zipping quickly up her spine. *I've never felt anything else like it in my life.*

They'd spent hours and hours together—even a night on the beach in San Francisco talking until four in the morning. Adam had ended up spending the rest of that night with her in her hotel room, and it had been everything she could do not to make love with him.

On her way back to Sunset Island, she'd been overwhelmed with guilt and remorse and had decided that she'd fallen so hard for Adam because Kurt had been pressing her for a commitment she hadn't been ready to make. *But I am ready now,* she told herself adamantly. *In fact, I've already made the commitment. But why does the very sound of Adam's voice send me right back to how it felt to be in his arms?*

"Emma? Are you there?" Adam called into the phone.

"I'm here," Emma replied. "I . . . I didn't expect to hear from you."

"Why not?" Adam asked. "I told you what we had was more than some stupid fling— but then, you already knew that."

"Yes, but I told you I was in love with Kurt and I still am—" Emma said. *Does he know I'm getting married?* Emma wondered. *Why is it so hard to tell him?*

"Sam told me," Adam said quietly, as if he had been reading her mind.

"It's true," Emma said, gripping the phone harder. She made herself say the words. "Kurt and I are getting married. In less than two weeks."

"Can I be in the wedding party?" Adam joked. "I bet he'd be surprised if you made me one of the groomsmen."

Emma laughed in spite of herself. Adam always made her laugh—always had a sense of humor about even the most serious things.

It's one of the things I like so much about him! she remembered.

"Emma," Adam murmured, his voice turning husky and serious, "please don't do this. Please reconsider. It's not too late."

"It is too late," Emma insisted. "I already said yes. And I love him."

"You could love me," Adam said earnestly. "You know you could if we gave it some time—"

"That doesn't make any sense," Emma said, cutting him off. "What we had . . . look, you're right, it was special. It wasn't just a fling. But . . . things have changed. I've made a commitment."

"You're too young to get married!"

"No, I'm not," Emma said flatly.

"You hardly know him! Not even two years!"

"I know him enough to know I love him," Emma answered. "I know him better than I know you."

"In some ways," Adam agreed. "But in some ways not."

"Please," Emma begged, "don't make this harder for me than it already is."

"But don't you see, it shouldn't be hard," Adam insisted. "If it's hard there's something wrong, something you're not facing! It should be joy, and happiness, and—"

"Did Sam tell you why I'm doing this now?" Emma interrupted Adam.

"Something about the Peace Corps and a car accident," Adam said quietly.

"That's right," Emma responded, running her fingers through her hair nervously. "I'm going to Africa this fall—I hope."

"Great," Adam said, "you should absolutely do what your heart tells you to do. But, God, Emma, you should go single, not married."

"Since when do you know what I should do?" Emma asked, fighting for self-control.

"Because I love you, dammit!" Adam yelled.

"Oh, Adam, you don't even know me—"

"That's not true," Adam insisted. "I can't get you out of my mind. Can you honestly tell me you never think about me?"

"No," Emma admitted in a small voice.

"Don't throw that away—"

"Adam, please, this is so unfair of you!" Emma cried into the phone. "If you really care about me, you should just be glad that I'm happy and in love—"

Adam interrupted again. "I guess it's just that I hoped . . ."

Hoped that he and I would get a chance to get to know each other better, hoped that we would fall in love and be together, Emma thought to herself. *Do I dare tell him that late at night, when I allow myself to think my deepest thoughts, I've dreamed that, too?*

"Adam, I'm sorry," Emma said with finality.

"I'm sorry, too," Adam murmured quietly. "I've never met anyone like you before in my life. And I feel like we're just throwing love away."

Oh, God, Emma thought, *why does this have to be so hard? Am I crazy to still have these feelings for him? He used the exact words I used about Kurt. . . .*

"Maybe . . . maybe if we'd met each other at another time, in another place," Emma admitted, her voice an intimate whisper into the phone. "But . . . we didn't."

"No, we didn't," Adam agreed sadly. "But doesn't the way you feel about me make you think you should reconsider?"

"No." Emma felt her resolve return. "I love Kurt, and I could never, ever hurt him like that. Sometimes you have to make decisions to be an adult. I'm not turning back."

Silence.

"Nice speech," Adam said with some attempt at lightening his tone. "So, is there any chance that you'll put me in the wedding party?"

"Oh, Adam," Emma said, a sad smile on her lips.

"Life's nuts," Adam stated.

"You're right," Emma agreed.

"Just make sure you're picking the right person to go crazy with, then," Adam advised her.

"I'm sure," Emma responded quickly.

"Then send me a card from your honeymoon," Adam suggested.

"I'll do that," Emma agreed, though she had no intention of doing any such thing.

"Well, I guess there isn't anything left to say," Adam said. "Good luck, Emma. I'll never forget you."

"I feel the same way," she admitted.

"Good-bye," Adam whispered, and the phone went dead in her hand.

"Good-bye," she said to the thin air. "Good-bye, Adam."

She replaced the phone and just sat there, staring at the wall. She didn't realize that goosebumps covered her still-wet body, or that she was staring into space. And for about the zillionth time she thought: *Why does it all have to be so hard?*

126

*　　*　　*

"That Lord Owen guy has got to go," Kurt said to Emma. It was an hour later, and they were on their way to the travel agency to discuss their honeymoon. As far as Emma was concerned, it was the last thing on her mind, but she tried for a quick attitude adjustment. *After all, it's not Kurt's fault if I'm immature and fickle,* Emma thought.

"But he really is helping," Emma said.

There was a lot of traffic on Shore Road because people were leaving the beach, and Kurt's car—his old one, now repaired—just barely inched along.

"He's a supercilious jerk," Kurt stated. "He treats me like I'm five years old!"

"It's just his way of trying to pretend he's superior—it's all an act," Emma explained.

"A very bad act," Kurt said sourly.

"Well, he's supposed to be the best," Emma replied. "Try to put up with his moods."

"Moods?" Kurt replied archly. "He has two moods: nasty and intolerable."

Emma laughed. From her upbringing in tony Boston, she was used to characters like Lord Owen—who were usually entirely harmless. Obviously, Kurt was not.

"He's already done a ton of work," Emma said. "I'd be a basket case without his help."

"I doubt it," Kurt replied. "Who ever heard of anyone who was a professional wedding planner, anyway? Who needs it?"

"We do," Emma responded, as they finally turned down Main Street. "When you're starting as late as we are, you need help."

"With help like him, who needs enemies?" Kurt grumbled.

"Try to be nice to him," Emma asked. "Please. He'll be out of our lives forever in less than two weeks."

Kurt made a face. "I'll try," he said, as he pulled the car into Sunset Travel's small parking lot just off of Main Street.

The proprietor, Mrs. Hudson, was standing at the door to greet them. Like almost everyone who worked year-round on the island, she knew Kurt and his family, and as she ushered Kurt and Emma into her tiny office, she reminisced with him about some band concert she had seen when he was eleven years old where Kurt had played the cymbals and had dropped one of them in the middle of a song.

"So," Kurt grinned, "I'm not perfect."

"Perfect enough for me," Emma assured him, hugging his arm fiercely. *I really do love him so much*, Emma thought to herself. *It's only when I'm not with him that I have those stupid doubts. When I'm with him, I'm the happiest girl on earth.*

"Golly, but I love planning honeymoons," Mrs. Hudson said. "Always such a pleasure. So, what did you two lovebirds have in mind?"

Emma and Kurt looked at each other. This was another one of the topics that they had never broached—things were happening so fast that they just didn't get around to talking about honeymoons.

"Well, we haven't really had time to discuss it," Emma said, slowly.

"So, let's talk about it now!" Mrs. Hudson cried. "Jeepers, what fun! I get to be in on your plans!" She was one of those people who was enthusiastic about everything.

Kurt looked at Emma expectantly. When she didn't say anything, he spoke up.

"Well," he said, "I've always had a dream honeymoon in mind, ever since I was a teen."

I wonder what it could be? Emma thought to herself, beginning to get excited about her honeymoon after all. *A cruise around the world? Two weeks on an island in the South Pacific? A safari in Africa? Any of those things would be great with me. I want my honeymoon to be a romantic adventure!*

"So," Mrs. Hudson prompted, "let's hear it!"

Kurt's eyes got dreamy. "I love my own state so much," he murmured. "I'd always dreamed about renting a four-wheel drive and just bombing around Maine for a couple of weeks."

Oh, my God, he's joking, Emma thought, dumbfounded.

Kurt briefly looked over at her and took Emma's continued silence for agreement. He pressed on.

"It'd be great," he continued with enthusiasm. "We could stay in some inns, do some camping, go fishing on the Moose River, climb Mount Katahdin, even go out to Eastport to watch the sunrise."

"Jeepers, that's a great honeymoon!" Mrs. Hudson agreed. "Don't you think that's a fabulous honeymoon?" The two of them looked at Emma.

Emma looked at Mrs. Hudson, then she looked at Kurt, then she looked back at Mrs. Hudson again. "Could you excuse us for a moment, please?" she asked politely, trying to keep the ice out of her voice.

"Of course!" Mrs. Hudson said, her tone still gay. "You lovebirds just chat as long as you need to!" She got up and left the room.

Emma turned and faced Kurt.

"Fishing on the Moose River?" she asked him, archly.

"It'd be great," he maintained. "The trout bite all summer long."

"Kurt," Emma replied, "I don't know how to break this to you, but I have no interest in fishing and our honeymoon is not going to include the Moose River."

"But—"

"In fact," Emma continued, "our honeymoon is not going to happen in the state of Maine."

"But that's something we can afford!" Kurt cried.

"Kurt, you're missing the larger picture here," Emma almost shouted. "We can afford anything. Anything! Money is not the issue!"

"Yes, it is!"

"No, it's not!" Emma maintained irritably. "This is supposed to be the greatest trip of our lives! It's our honeymoon! It should be romantic, loving, exotic . . ."

"Just stop right there," Kurt said. "You are not going to pay for our honeymoon, and that is final."

"Haven't you ever heard of presents?" Emma said hotly. "Some people like to give them at weddings!"

"What does that have to do with anything?" Kurt asked.

"My father!" Emma replied. "My father's sending us on our honeymoon! He told me! We can go anywhere we want!"

Kurt visibly relaxed.

"Oh," he said, a little more calmly. "That changes things."

"It should," Emma sniffed.

Is this going to happen all the time? she asked herself. *Anytime we're going to do something that costs more than five dollars, is Kurt going to hold it against me?*

"Well," Kurt said easily, "what did you have in mind?"

"A trip," Emma responded. "A romantic trip." Though at the moment she felt something less than romantic.

"Just a sec," Kurt said, and went to get Mrs. Hudson back into the room. She came in smiling and sat down at her desk.

"So will it be a tour of Maine?" she asked excitedly.

"No, Paris," Emma responded firmly. "A week in Paris, France—maybe a Left Bank hotel?—and a week on the Mediterranean in Spain—maybe Marbella."

Mrs. Hudson whistled. "Jeepers, golly, well, gee-wiz!" She looked doubtfully at Kurt. "I can arrange that, if you want?"

"Then do it, please," Kurt said, rising to his feet. "Call me as soon as you have some more information."

"Oh, fine," Mrs. Hudson replied. "Golly, what a honeymoon! I'm thrilled just planning it!" She got out a pad of paper. "So, when is the wedding and when is the big trip?"

"The wedding is a week from Sunday," Emma said.

"Jeepers!" Mrs. Hudson cried, her eyes checking out Emma's flat stomach.

Emma stood up. This time she just couldn't help herself. "Jeepers!" she yelled. "I am not pregnant!" She marched out of the travel agency.

Kurt followed her, a smile playing around his lips. "Jeepers, I'm not pregnant?" he quoted Emma.

"Sorry, but everyone keeps staring at my stomach because we're getting married so quickly."

Kurt burst out laughing. "It would have to be the immaculate conception!"

Emma laughed, too. "I know," she agreed as they reached the car.

He held open the car door for her. "Come on, there's something I want to show you."

Emma got in the car as Kurt went around to the driver's side.

"I know I shouldn't have marched out of her office," Emma said contritely. "That isn't even like me!"

"Don't worry about it, Em. You're allowed to be in a bad mood now and then." Kurt leaned over and kissed Emma's cheek, then he started the car.

"She'll take care of the trip?" Emma asked Kurt anxiously.

"Hasn't failed my family yet," Kurt responded as he pulled the car out of the parking lot.

"Good—"

"On the other hand, I've never had her book us anything more than a bus ticket to Wiscasset," Kurt said wryly, turning on to Shore Road.

Emma laughed and leaned her head against Kurt's arm.

Everything is going to be fine.

Kurt unfolded the blanket he kept in his trunk and plopped down on it on one of the dunes overlooking the ocean. He reached up for Emma, took her hand, and she lay down beside him on the blanket. The spot was about four miles from Main Street and very secluded. Now, it was just Kurt, Emma, the dunes, the ocean, and the setting sun.

"Nice," Emma commented, snuggling next to Kurt.

"Nothing's too nice for my wife-to-be," Kurt smiled.

"Wife-to-be," Emma marveled. "I'm still getting used to that."

"I'll be getting used to it for about five years," Kurt joked.

"I'm looking forward to it," Emma said, a little shyly.

"Me, too," Kurt answered.

"Show me how much," Emma said boldly.

"This much," Kurt said, and leaned forward to kiss her.

Emma tilted her head back and closed her eyes, expecting to feel the touch of Kurt's lips on hers.

It never happened.

She opened her eyes and looked at Kurt, puzzled.

"What's wrong?" she asked.

"Nothing," Kurt said, his eyes shining in the orange dusky light.

"You were going to show me how much," Emma reminded him sexily.

"I am," Kurt murmured, his face still shining. "Look."

Emma followed Kurt's nod down to the blanket.

There, on the blanket, on a square of black felt, was the most gorgeous diamond ring Emma had ever seen. She'd seen bigger rings, bolder rings, showier rings, but never one as beautiful as this one. It was a solitaire perfect-cut diamond—it looked to Emma like about a carat—in an antique setting, surrounded by three smaller diamonds on each side.

The day Kurt had gotten his mother's ring out of the safe deposit box, he'd sized Emma's left ring finger. When he'd discovered that his mother's ring was too big, he'd insisted on taking it to a jeweler to have it fitted to Emma's size before he gave it to her. And now, here it was.

"Wow," Emma said. "Wow. It's magnificent," she said simply, picking it up.

"Allow me," Kurt said gallantly, taking the ring out of Emma's hand, and then slipping it onto the fourth finger of her left hand.

Emma gazed at it, speechless.

"Fits pretty good," Kurt commented with a grin. "Like it was made for you."

"I love you," Emma said simply. "I love you, Kurt Ackerman."

"Show me how much," Kurt replied, echoing Emma's words of a few moments before.

"You show me," Emma teased in a sexy voice.

He did.

TEN

"Can I see your wedding ring?" Katie shyly asked Emma at the breakfast table the next morning.

"Of course you can see it, sweetie," Emma told her, holding her hand out for inspection. "But it's not called a wedding ring. It's called an engagement ring. I don't get the wedding ring until the day of the wedding."

Katie held Emma's hand in her tiny pudgy one and inspected the ring. "It's beautiful," she said. "Did you give Kurt an engagement ring?"

"No," Emma said, "but I will give him a wedding ring." *One more thing on my endless list,* she reminded herself. *I have to find wedding rings!*

"Someday I'll get one," Katie said solemnly.

"Right," Emma agreed, "when you get married."

"Hey, let's get you an education first, kiddo," Jane Hewitt said cheerfully from the stove where she was making scrambled eggs.

"Are you sure you don't want any help with that?" Emma asked. "I feel like I haven't been doing anything around here lately."

"Well, you haven't," Jane said with laughter in her voice. "But I think you're plenty busy enough trying to pull off this two-week-miracle wedding."

"I can do more—" Emma began guiltily.

"Hey, it's fine, Emma, honest," Jane assured her. "It isn't every day we have a bride in the family."

Emma felt a tightening in her throat. She loved Jane—the whole Hewitt family—so much. *They really have made me like a member of their family*, Emma realized. *I'm going to miss being a part of them. . . .*

"After you get married can you still live with us?" Katie asked, climbing up on to Emma's lap.

"No, honey," Emma said. "Once I'm married I'm going to live with Kurt."

"Where?" Katie wondered.

Good question, Emma thought. *Kurt wants us to live with his dad and his sisters until I leave for the Peace Corps. Not that I've even heard from the Peace Corps to know if they've accepted me. Help! Everything is happening too fast!*

"Uh, we haven't actually decided yet," Emma replied.

"Hi," Ethan said, coming into the kitchen. He poured himself some orange juice. "Uh, did you see that letter from the Peace Corps?" he asked Emma.

Her heart sped up in her chest. "No, but it's too early for the mail to have arrived. "Where is it?"

"Well, uh, it might have, um . . . come yesterday," Ethan admitted sheepishly. "And I might have stuck it in my pocket and forgot to give it to you." He reached into his back pocket and handed the envelope to Emma.

"Thanks," Emma said. "Well, it certainly is from the Peace Corps," she said, reading the return address. "I'm nervous," she told Jane.

"Me, too, but open it anyway," Jane said, coming over to the table.

Emma opened the envelope and quickly read the letter inside.

Dear Ms. Cresswell,
We have received your application for the Peace Corps. It is being processed at this time. We note your first choice is Africa, and that you would prefer a situation in which you can study or work with primates. We have only one assignment that would fit this description, which involves teaching and doing research in the country of Zaire. We assume this would be

your first choice assignment.

Because of your language proficiency, we would also be interested in your considering an assignment in the Cameroon, for which we require bilingual workers. However, this assignment would not involve work with primates.

You will hear from us as soon as your application is completely processed. Thank you for your commitment to the Peace Corps.

"Does that mean I'm in?" Emma asked Jane.

"Well, they have to check everything on your application first, but it sounds to me like because of the fact that you speak five languages you've got a really good shot."

"I'd love to get sent to Zaire," Emma said, folding the letter and putting it back into the envelope.

"Well, maybe you will," Jane said, going back to her eggs.

"God, Jane, it doesn't seem real—talking about going to Africa, getting married . . ."

"Your life is changing pretty fast," Jane agreed. "It's kind of scary, huh?"

Emma nodded. "Overwhelming, really."

The front doorbell rang.

"I'm sure that's Carrie and Sam," Emma said. "You sure you don't need me?" Emma asked, getting up from the table.

"Emma, chill!" Jane instructed. "I honestly don't expect you to do much between now and the wedding. And it's fine."

"Thanks," Emma said gratefully, and went to get the door.

"The rock, the rock, we want to see the rock!" Sam screeched, grabbing for Emma's left hand.

Emma held it out proudly.

"Oh, Emma it's beautiful," Carrie breathed, holding Emma's hand in hers.

"Thanks," Emma said with a small smile.

"Whoa, one big mother diamond and a lot of little baby diamonds," Sam said, turning Emma's hand so that the stones glinted under the morning light. "It's too cool."

"Let's go in the backyard," Emma suggested. "I can go over all the stuff Lord Owen and I have done so far. I spent two hours with him last night—he's relentless."

Outside, Sam plopped down into the hammock. "Okay, give us the list," she said.

Emma sat on the redwood bench. "Well, the photographer is all set—"

"It's Flash Hathaway!" Sam cried. "I know it's Flash!"

"No," Emma said with a laugh, "but it is someone you know," she said, looking at Carrie.

"Who?" Carrie asked, a puzzled look on her face.

"David Frohman!" Emma cried. "Lord Owen actually got David Frohman!"

The girls had all met Pulitzer Prize–winning photographer David Frohman and his chic wife, Edine, at a gallery showing on the island. He was by far Carrie's favorite photographer.

"Unbelievable!" Carrie exclaimed. "Whatever bad stuff I've been thinking about Lord Owen, I take back. I can't believe he's getting David Frohman to photograph your wedding! I mean, David Frohman doesn't usually do weddings!"

"I know, it's incredible," Emma agreed. "Oh, and listen to this menu." She opened her notebook and read off a list. "Caviar and Moet & Chandon champagne, various hors d'ouevres including imported smoked salmon, fois gras, cold Maine lobster, shrimp and crayfish, and that is just for the milling-around part before the dinner—"

"You're making me hungry!" Sam said with a laugh. "Tell us more!"

"Okay, the sit-down dinner menu is vichyssoise topped with sour cream and caviar—"

"Caviar is disgusting," Sam interrupted.

"You've only had it once, at the art gallery!" Carrie reminded her.

"I know, and it was so gross!" Sam said with a shudder. "All those little dead fish eggs crunching under my teeth—"

"Ignore her and continue," Carrie advised.

"Lobster and wild mushrooms in puff pastry, endive and goat cheese salad vinaigrette," Emma read, "a choice of prime rib or pheasant under glass with appropriate side dishes, and of course there's sorbet between each course to cleanse the palette," Emma continued.

"Cleanse the palette?" Sam broke in. "Gimme a break!"

"Followed by wedding cake—which is a Belgian torte being flown in from Belgium—"

"You're kidding," Carrie said.

"I'm not," Emma insisted. "Along with that, various exotic fresh fruits, imported chocolate and petits fours, and four different kinds of coffee. And, oh, of course, appropriate wine with each course."

"Oh, of course," Carrie echoed solemnly.

"Gee, no cheeseburgers?" Sam asked. She launched herself from the hammock. "That menu is unbelievable. Who's catering all that?"

"Some of it is coming from the caterers who do affairs at the Sunset Inn," Emma said. "But Lord Owen has various people flying in from various places—I'm sort of leaving all of it in his hands."

"Who says money can't buy happiness?" Sam said with a sigh. She sat down next to Emma. "Not to change the subject or anything, but I

143

was wondering if you got any kind of . . . special phone call?"

"You mean Adam," Emma said. "You knew he was going to call me?"

"Well, he kind of told me was going to," Sam admitted. "I couldn't really stop him or anything."

Carrie looked surprised. "Adam called you?" she asked Emma.

"Yes," Emma said, closing her wedding notebook.

"Was it difficult?" Carrie asked.

"No," she said quickly. "It was fine."

Her friends stared at her.

"I'm lying," Emma blurting out. "It was awful." She buried her head in her hands. "You guys, I feel like I'm losing my mind! One minute I'm so happy I want to jump around and shout like a maniac, and the next minute I want to run away so far and so fast that no one can ever find me!"

"Maybe that's how everyone feels when they're planning their wedding," Carrie commiserated.

Emma raised her anxious face. "You think so?"

"I don't know," Carrie admitted.

"So, what did Adam say, exactly?" Sam asked.

"He said he loves me," Emma said in a low voice.

"Whoa Baby!" Sam exclaimed. "You've got two guys in love with you and I haven't even got a date!"

144

"Would you please be serious for a few minutes?" Carrie asked Sam. "This is tough for Emma."

"I know," Sam agreed. "Sorry." She tapped the tips of her cowboy boots against each other. "Is it making you have second thoughts?"

"No," Emma said adamantly. "I would never do that to Kurt."

"Don't think about Kurt right now," Carrie said firmly. "Think about you."

"I love Kurt!" Emma protested. "I hardly know Adam!"

"But you still sound confused," Carrie pointed out gently.

"No!" Emma insisted, jumping up from the bench. "I'm not confused, and I am getting married. And that is that!"

Neither Carrie or Sam dared to say a word.

It was that evening, and Emma was getting ready for Kurt to come pick her up. They planned to go for a walk along the beach so they could talk about the wedding, then maybe go out for something to eat.

Emma opened her lingerie drawer and selected her favorite pale pink silk teddy with the delicate lace around the neckline and the legs. She slipped it on and stared at herself in the mirror. *I do love Kurt*, she told her reflection. She closed her eyes, wrapped her arms around herself and thought about the feel of his arms, his lips. She wanted them to feel so close, so committed, without any of the doubts that had been assailing her. Suddenly her eyes popped open.

I know just what to do! Emma thought with excitement. *I know why we keep fighting! It's because we're two adults in love with each other, about to be married, who are still just making out like a pair of silly teenagers! It's stupid, it's juvenile! Once Kurt and I become lovers, everything will be fine!*

She smiled at her reflection in the mirror. Her eyes sparkled with anticipation. *This is absolutely the right thing to do,* she thought exultantly. *Oh, Kurt, my darling, tonight is the night that we finally give ourselves to each other completely, and then all this silly bickering will end!*

She carefully sprayed herself with her best French perfume, slipped into a long, feminine white lace skirt, and buttoned a white crocheted open-weave sweater over her teddy. She pulled on her white sandals, put on some light makeup, and surveyed her image in the mirror.

"Emma Cresswell," she told her reflection, "tonight is the night you will finally know what it's like to make love."

ELEVEN

Emma held her white sandals in one hand and Kurt's hand in the other, as the two of them strolled leisurely down the beach. She looked at Kurt out of the corner of her eye. He had on faded jeans and a red rugby shirt, and he carried a worn jean jacket over his shoulder. His sun-streaked brownish-blond hair was ruffled by the ocean breeze. *He is so handsome*, she thought, a smile playing on her lips. *And tonight is going to be so very, very special. Not that he knows it yet.*

"I was wondering," Kurt said. "I know you don't know my sisters very well, but . . . I'd really like it if they could be in the wedding party."

Emma thought about it for a second. "That would be fine," she decided. "They'd need to go to the Bridal Shoppe in Portland and pick up dresses to match Sam and Carrie's."

"That's cool," Kurt assured her. "And you

want little Katie to be the flower girl?"

Emma nodded. "Jane bought her the cutest dress—it's baby pink with a huge bow at the back, and underneath it is a white lace petticoat that sticks out on the bottom. Katie begged to sleep in it tonight!"

Kurt smiled. He'd been Katie's swimming instructor for the last two summers, and Katie had always had a crush on him. "She's a really cute kid." He looked over at Emma. "You think someday we'll have a little girl that cute?"

"Cuter," Emma said decisively. "And a little boy who looks just like you."

"Only shorter," Kurt added with a laugh.

They walked a ways without speaking, enjoying the feeling of the cool sand squishing between their toes. Emma could just make out a gull circling the sky in the fading light. "You know, you haven't said what guys you want as your groomsmen," Emma reminded Kurt.

Maybe I can be in the wedding, Emma heard Adam tell her in her mind. She banished the memory as quickly possible. *I refuse to think about him. He is in the past.*

"I wanted to talk to you about that," Kurt said. "Jason Levine is my closest friend from the pool," Kurt said, naming the new assistant aquatics director. "I'd like to ask him. And I'd like to have my first cousin, Freddie—you haven't met him yet, because he's away at the University of Michigan. But the two of us grew up together—he's really my best friend. I called him and he said he could fly in—actually he said he wouldn't miss it. And I want to have Billy and Pres."

Emma smiled at him. "I was hoping you'd ask Billy and Pres."

"I will," Kurt said. "But I wanted to run it by you. Will Sam freak out about it, since she and Pres broke up?"

"Actually, I asked her," Emma reported, "just in case you were planning to ask Pres. She thinks it's a great idea."

"Really?" Kurt asked with surprise.

Emma nodded. "She wants him back, you know. She said she's hoping that the wedding will be so romantic he'll appreciate her all over again and fall into her arms."

"Anything is possible," Kurt said. "He still really cares about her."

"I know that," Emma agreed. "Sam is just so scared of making a commitment. . . ."

Kurt turned to Emma. "Aren't you glad you're not?" he said softly.

"Very glad," she answered, and wrapped her arms around his neck.

She kissed him softly at first, then more fully. Kurt held her waist and pulled her closer, escalating the passion of their kisses.

Emma pulled her face away from Kurt's

for a moment. They were at a very deserted section of the beach. "Put your jacket down," Emma whispered.

Wordlessly Kurt threw his jacket down on the sand, and Emma sat down on it, lifting her arms to Kurt. He knelt over her, lovingly kissing her hair, her face, and finally her lips. With all the love and passion she felt, Emma returned his kisses and caresses, until both of them were breathless with desire.

Slowly Emma sat up and unbuttoned her white sweater, letting it fall off her shoulders. Her pale pink teddy gleamed under the golden light of the full moon.

"Emma," Kurt said huskily, and took her in his arms again. He kissed her neck, down to her collarbone, slipping the thin strap off her shoulder.

"Kurt, I love you," Emma whispered fiercely.

"I love you, too, so much," Kurt said returning his kisses to her mouth.

Well, it's now or never, Emma told herself. *I know this is the right thing to do. Love makes everything all right, and making love will bind us together so that I won't have any doubts, ever again. We'll have to stop for condoms in an all-night drug-store. But after that we can go right to the Sunset Inn. All I have to do is tell him that I want him now. . . .*

"Kurt? Darling?" Emma whispered.

"Mmmmmmm?" Kurt said, kissing slowly down to her cleavage.

"Let's . . . let's go get a hotel room."

Kurt stopped kissing her and searched her face with his eyes. "You mean—?"

"Yes," Emma said fervently. "I want us to make love. I want you to make love to me." She felt shy saying it, but reminded herself that he was her fiancé now, that she had every right to want him and need him to love her.

Tenderly Kurt pushed some hair behind Emma's ear. "Are you sure?"

"I'm sure," Emma told him.

He was silent for a moment. "It's just . . ." He laughed quickly. "God, I've dreamt so many times about having you finally say that to me, and now—"

"And now what?" Emma asked, rising up on her elbows.

"And now . . . well . . . now I think we should wait until we're married," Kurt said slowly.

Emma suddenly felt chilled, and she pulled her sweater around her shoulders. "But . . . I'm always the one who's stopped us from going further—"

"I know," Kurt said. "And believe me, I want you so badly that sometimes I've thought I could die."

"Then I don't understand—" Emma began.

"I don't either," Kurt put in. "I guess..." He sat back and stared up the starry night sky, searching for words. "I guess I figure the best way I can really prove to you how much I love you is to wait and make love to you when I've made that final commitment."

"But maybe if we make love we'll feel even closer," Emma said. "No ceremony is going to magically make us feel any more in love, or any more committed."

"For me, Em, standing up in front of my family and our friends and, well, in front of God, and taking solemn vows to be your husband all the days of my life—yeah, that changes things."

Emma was quiet for a moment, thinking about what Kurt said, and then she laughed. "Who would have thought that you'd ever turn me down?"

Kurt gently pushed Emma back down on his jacket, and he moved over her. "I'm not turning you down, my love, I'm just... putting us on hold."

"What if it turns out we're not sexually compatible?" Emma asked.

This time Kurt laughed. "Do you think that's possible?"

Kurt kissed Emma again, and everything inside of her melted.

Well, so much for Sam's theory about look-

ing under the hood and taking it for a test drive, Emma thought giddily. *Just this once I'm going to have to rely on truth in advertising!*

"Good morning, Emma, how are we feeling today?" Lord Owen greeted Emma as she joined him at his breakfast table outside on the main deck of the Sunset Inn the next morning.

"Fine," Emma replied, surveying the typically British breakfast of tea, toast, and kippers he'd ordered.

"Would we care for some tea?" he offered, uncharacteristically generous.

"That would be nice," Emma said, sitting down opposite him.

"Our waiter should be along in a moment," Lord Owen said. "You can order it then." He flipped open his notebook. "Our work continues, even at meals."

"Um-hum," Emma replied noncommittally.

Lord Owen took a long sip of tea and closed his eyes with bliss. "We bring the tea with us from London, of course. Your tea reminds us of dunking athletic socks in warm water," he said. "Unfortunately, we did not bring tea for two to breakfast," he added unctuously.

"Would you like to order, miss?" the waiter asked, hovering over the table.

"A cup of tea, please," Emma ordered.

"Anything to eat?" the young waiter asked.

"No, just tea will be fine," Emma told him.

He grinned at her and walked away.

"So," Lord Owen said, scanning his list, "let us discuss a religious leader."

"What?" Emma replied, totally baffled.

"We are?" Lord Owen asked, his pen poised.

"We are what?" Emma asked.

"Our faith is?" Lord Owen elucidated.

"I don't understand," Emma said honestly.

"Affiliation, church, that sort of thing," Lord Owen prompted. "Protestant? Episcopalian? Some quaint Quaker group?"

"I'm Episcopalian," Emma reported, finally catching on. "Kurt's family is Unitarian."

"Ah, that's nice," Lord Owen said, taking another sip of tea and flipping to a computer printout he had in one of his notebooks.

"What's that?" Emma asked.

"We have here a list of available clergy, taken from a computer database in Boston," Lord Owen reported.

"Uh, excuse me," Emma said, "Kurt and I are planning to write our own vows. In fact, mine are already written."

"Quaint," Lord Owen replied. "So very quaint. Now, I suggest we toss those vows directly into the rubbish and begin to plan your ceremony."

I'm sorry, but this is one subject that I am

154

not going to budge on, Emma thought to herself. *This one we are going to do our way.*

"After all," Lord Owen continued, as if he was talking to a third person and not to Emma, "Emma is a Cresswell. Cresswells are not married by mayors and justices of the peace. It simply is not done."

"Wrong," Emma said firmly. She put on her best Kat Cresswell expression. *If he wants supercilious, I'll give him supercilious,* Emma thought defiantly. "Since I am a Cresswell, you know that a Cresswell gets what a Cresswell wants. In fact, Judge Easton is going to marry us. Kurt already checked."

Lord Owen eyed Emma coolly for a moment, then he picked up another notebook and began flipping through it. "Ah, Judge Easton, yes, here he is." Lord Owen looked up at Emma. "We are referring to Judge Thomas Easton, of Sunset Island Criminal Court?"

"That's him," Emma said brightly. "He's an old family friend of the Ackermans and—"

"Criminal court, that's somehow appropriate," Lord Owen said dryly. "Perhaps there are a few actual criminals you and your beloved would like to invite in to the ceremony for some local color."

Emma stared Lord Owen in the eye. "Judge Easton is performing the ceremony, and Kurt and I are writing our own vows."

"Very good," Lord Owen said, in a voice that

meant it wasn't very good at all. "Make a mockery of the institution, why don't we? Let's move on to music. Is Judge Easton going to play the fiddle and spoons, as well?"

"I was thinking along the lines of a band," Emma replied, refusing to let Lord Owen get to her.

"Capital idea," Lord Owen said. "Any particular band, since we seem to have such strong opinions? No, let me guess. Perhaps after our original ceremony, we would like to be entertained by the Grateful Dead?"

The waiter brought Emma her tea and slipped away.

She poured from the small pot of steeping tea into her cup. "I was thinking something a bit more traditional," she said evenly.

"Oh, super-goody," Lord Owen said blithely. He opened to his first notebook again. "We've taken the liberty of engaging a string quartet to play before the ceremony, a harpist during the early courses of the meal, and Harry Connick, Jr., for the main reception."

Emma stopped with her cup halfway to her mouth. "You really got Harry Connick, Jr.?"

Lord Owen slipped his sunglasses out of his pocket and put them on. "We never promise that which we can not deliver," he said.

"Well, that's . . . that's fabulous," Emma had to admit.

"Now, for the guest list," Lord Owen continued. "I have, of course, the lists you and Kurt provided, and this morning I received a fax from your parents with their guest list."

He showed the list to Emma. She looked down at the bottom and saw the number 322.

"They're kidding," Emma said flatly.

"We realize, of course, that if Mr. and Mrs. Cresswell had more time, the list would be somewhat longer," Lord Owen mused, "but we will have to make do, won't we?"

"Over three hundred people is simply out of the question!" Emma exclaimed. "I only had forty names on my list, and Kurt only had thirty-three on his!"

"Yes, quite," Lord Owen agreed.

"Well, don't you see?" Emma asked. "It would be horrible! Kurt's side would have thirty-three people, and my side would have three hundred something!"

"The imbalance is staggering," Lord Owen agreed. "But then, we assume we knew what we were getting into when we decided to marry Curtis, did we not?"

"It's Kurt, not Curtis," Emma snapped. "Look, you'll just have to call my mother and tell her no."

"But—"

"No, I mean it," Emma insisted vehemently. "Tell her her she and Dad are limited to one hundred guests, and I mean it."

Lord Owen cleared his throat. "Is that quite gracious when our parents are giving us this wedding?" he pointed out.

Emma's shoulder's sagged. "I forgot about that," she admitted. She sipped at her tea. "All right. Tell her one hundred and fifty."

"Is a hundred and fifty somehow more gracious than one hundred?" Lord Owen asked with an arched brow.

"Tell her . . . oh, tell her to do whatever she wants," Emma snapped. "She will, anyway."

"An excellent decision," Lord Owen agreed, checking it off his list. "Also, since it would be terribly gauche to print and mail invitations at this late date, we will arrange for all parties to be telephoned, which will be followed up with a telegram. I assume that is satisfactory. Now, as for your bridal gown, yesterday I arranged for twenty gowns by the very top bridal gown designers to be sent in by Federal Express from New York—"

"I've got a gown," Emma said quickly.

Okay, so I'm lying, Emma thought. *I just can't stand the way he takes everything over all the time!*

"We have a gown?" Lord Owen asked.

"No, *I* have a gown," Emma corrected him, "unless of course you were planning to wear one, too."

"Well, well," Lord Owen said, "we show some unexpected initiative. What color is it?"

"White," Emma said, deadpan.

"Goody," Lord Owen replied, "white wedding gowns are so chic this year. When will we see this Emma-chosen gown?"

"The day of the wedding," Emma replied firmly.

"I see," Lord Owen said. He rolled his eyes heavenward and checked it off his list. "And Master Curtis' formalwear?" Lord Owen asked.

"Kurt," Emma corrected him.

"Ah, yes, Kurt," Lord Owen repeated.

"He's renting it," Emma reported.

"We're *leasing*?" Lord Owen asked, in the same tone he would have used if he had just been told that Kurt was planning to be married in his birthday suit.

"Yes," Emma said, "we're leasing. But you'll be happy."

"Will I? Why is that?"

"It's a very short-term lease," Emma said gravely. "And we got a wonderful bargain."

"How so?" Lord Owen asked, archly.

"It was the only tie-dyed tuxedo they had left."

When Emma got back to the Hewitts' from her meeting, there was a telegram for her waiting on the kitchen counter. Several had arrived during the past few days, as her mother had obviously been spreading the word to her society friends around the country. Telegrams of congratulations seemed to be proper protocol this year.

Emma reached for it. *Adam,* she thought. *It's from Adam.* Her heart stopped for a moment. Then she tore open the wrapper.

What she read made her smile.

CONGRATS EMMA. BACK FROM EUROPE TO GET NEWS. IF YOU ARE HAPPY SO AM I. WILL BE WITH YOU FOR WEDDING. YOU AND KURT WILL BE GREAT. I CANNOT WAIT. LOVE, AUNT LIZ.

I love her. Why can't my mother be like her? Emma asked herself.

"Good news?" Jane asked, as she came into the kitchen and opened the refrigerator. "You're smiling."

"My Aunt Liz," Emma explained. "She's coming for the wedding."

"Great," Jane replied. "How's the planning coming?"

"It's endless," Emma admitted, falling into a chair at the breakfast table.

Jane got them both some juice and sat down. "Yeah, planning a wedding is a whole lot of work, even when you have six months or a year."

"Lord Owen is incredibly organized," Emma

admitted. "But I can't stand the man."

"Did you find yourself a gown yet?" Jane asked, sipping her juice.

Emma winced. "His Lordship was on my case about that again today."

"What did you tell him?"

"I lied and told him I had a gown," Emma admitted. "I just couldn't stand him anymore!"

"I'll go out and look with you, if that'll help," Jane offered.

Emma smiled at her gratefully. "Thanks, but I wouldn't even know where to look. I hate everything I see! They're all frilly and overdone. I can't stand that! And if they're not all overdone, they're so sophisticated that they belong on some bride in her thirties or something!"

"Too bad the two of us have the best taste on the planet!" she teased. Then something changed in her face. "I was just thinking . . ."

"What?" Emma asked.

"Well," Jane said hesitantly, choosing her words carefully, "I'd like to show you something."

"Sure," Emma replied.

"Wait here," Jane told her, as she got up from the kitchen table and went upstairs. Emma could hear the sounds of closets being opened and closed and boxes falling. Soon, though, Jane came back into the kitchen, carrying a box that was taped shut.

"What is it?" Emma asked, though she had a pretty good idea what it might be.

"Open it," Jane suggested, handing Emma a set of scissors. "Some of our stuff we actually store here instead of at the house in Portland, and luckily for me, this is one of those things."

Emma carefully cut the tape on the box and opened it.

And she couldn't believe her eyes.

In the box, nestled in tissue paper, was an absolutely gorgeous wedding dress.

She held it up. It was cream-colored, made from the finest silk she had ever seen. The neckline was cut straight across, shoulder to shoulder. The gown was cut close to the body on the bias, and then fell in rich folds to the floor. The only ornamentation was antique beadwork, clearly hand-sewn, that ran diagonally from just under the bust on the right side to the hem of the gown on the left.

"Wow!" Emma whispered. "Was this yours?"

"Yep." Jane grinned. "And the really amazing thing is that when I was married—that was about a century ago—I was just about your size."

"Wow."

"Try it on," Jane urged.

Emma stared at Jane, open-mouthed. "Oh, no, I couldn't—"

"Yes, please," Jane said. "No one else is home—you can slip into it right here. I'll run upstairs and get the veil—I just hope it didn't end up at the house in Portland."

Emma pulled off her cotton shirt and pants, and slipped into Jane's wedding gown. It fit her perfectly. Jane came back into the kitchen with an intricately woven veil the same color as the dress, with the beading pattern following the crown that held the veil. Jane smiled at Emma and very carefully put the veil on Emma's head.

"Go look in the mirror," Jane said to her.

Together they walked into the foyer, and Emma stood before the mirror.

"Oh, Jane," she whispered. *I look so beautiful,* she thought. Tears began to run down her cheeks.

"I think you've found your gown," Jane said softly. Then she started to cry, too. She put her arms around Emma, and the two of them wept together, careful not to have any tears fall on Jane's—now Emma's—perfect wedding gown.

TWELVE

"I can't believe you're really getting married in a week," Sam mused, as she and Emma found comfortable chaises by the main pool at the country club. "It doesn't seem real."

"I know," Emma agreed, putting her beach bag near the chaise. "I feel like it's all some kind of dream."

"Hey, Sam," Becky Jacobs said, running over to Sam. "See that cute guy over by Kurt?"

Sam sat up on the chaise and looked to where Becky was pointing. A very cute guy, about 5'8", with straight black hair and a lean, muscular build was talking with Kurt. "Yeah, what about him?" Sam asked.

Allie joined her identical twin sister. "We've never seen him before," she said. "And you know we make it our business to know every cute guy who comes to this pool."

"Never saw him before," Sam said, settling back down on the chaise.

"Oh-mi-God, oh-mi-God, Kurt and that guy

are coming this way!" Becky screeched, grabbing Allie's hand. "Act cool."

"I always act cool," Allie reminded her sister. "Besides, you're supposed to be in love with Ian Templeton."

"So?" Becky snapped at her sister. "I might be in love, but I'm not married."

Emma smiled. *No*, she thought, *but I almost am. Even though it doesn't seem real at all.*

"If you tell that guy we're only fourteen I will kill you," Allie hissed to Sam.

"Please," Sam muttered.

"Hi," Kurt said. "I want you guys to meet my cousin, Freddie Ackerman. He flew in from Ann Arbor for the wedding." Emma stood up and Kurt put his arm around her slender waist. "Freddie, this is Emma."

"Great to meet you," Freddie said with a big grin. "You're just as gorgeous as Kurt said you were."

"Thanks," Emma replied graciously.

"Uh-hum." Becky cleared her throat ostentatiously.

"I'm not ignoring you," Kurt told her with a laugh. "Freddie, the twins are Allie and Becky Jacobs, and this is one of Emma's best friends, Sam Bridges."

"Hi," Freddie said.

"So, you live in Michigan?" Becky asked, posing in what she obviously thought was a seductive pose in her skimpy red frilled bikini.

"Yeah, I'm a sophomore at the University of Michigan," he told her.

"Oh, yeah, college is cool," Allie said nonchalantly.

"Where do you go?" Freddie asked her.

"Uh, locally," Allie replied. "Want to go for a swim?"

"Sure," Freddie said. "Nice meeting you all—I hear this engagement party tonight is going to be a blast." He turned to walk to the pool with the twins.

"Hold on a sec," Becky said. She put her hands on her hips. "What engagement party?"

"In case it's any of your business," Sam said pointedly, "we're giving Kurt and Emma an engagement party on the beach tonight."

"I guess you meant to invite us but forgot," Allie said sweetly. "Anyway, we'd love to come."

Sam shot Allie a look, which Allie ignored.

"Come on, Freddie, wait till you see me do the dead man's float." Allie said. "I'm very buoyant." She took Freddie's hand, and he and the twins walked away.

"Don't worry," Sam told Emma and Kurt. "I'll make sure the twins don't crash the party tonight."

"Hey, can they help it if they look more like they're eighteen than fourteen?" Kurt said with a laugh. "Boy, wait till I tell Freddie!"

"Oh, I wanted to show you something," Emma remembered. She pulled a glossy pamphlet from her beach bag. "Those new apartments they built on Shore Road are starting to take applications, see?"

Kurt took the pamphlet from her but didn't look at it. "Honey, there doesn't seem to be any point in getting an apartment we'll live in only for a couple of months before you leave for the Peace Corps."

"I just won't be comfortable living with your family," Emma said in a low voice. "Besides, there really isn't any room for me."

"You'll move into my room," Kurt said easily.

Emma had a suffocating feeling. She'd seen Kurt's room—small, spare—with very, very thin walls.

"Kurt, we're getting married, not planning a . . . a weekend visit. It just won't work living at your dad's house!"

Kurt sighed and ran his fingers through his hair impatiently. "Emma, we'd have to sign a lease for an apartment, and leases are generally for at least six months, usually for a year. Now, I don't need that apartment after you're in Africa, and that means I'd break the lease."

"Well, so what?" Emma asked.

"You can't just break a lease, Emma," Kurt said evenly. "You have to pay if you break a lease."

"So what?" Emma said distinctly. "Kurt, we can afford to buy the entire apartment complex if we want to."

His face turned stony. "We'll discuss this later."

"Why, because you say so?" Emma asked. "You don't get to control our conversations."

"Just my part in them," Kurt said, "and I have to go back to work." He thrust the pamphlet back into Emma's hands, turned, and walked away.

Emma sat down hard on the chaise lounge. "Sometimes I could just kill him."

"Well, I could pretend I didn't hear a word, but that would be kind of dumb, wouldn't it?" Sam asked.

"Can you believe him?" Emma asked Sam.

Sam shrugged. "He's always been stubborn," she reminded Emma.

"This money thing is driving me nuts," Emma complained. "I understood how he didn't want to take my money when we were just dating, but we're getting married, and he's just as pig-headed about it as ever!"

"Well, it scares him," Sam said, turning over onto her stomach. "He's worried people will think he's marrying you for your bucks, I bet."

"That's ridiculous," Emma snapped. "He probably wishes I didn't have any money!"

"Maybe," Sam mused. "But maybe on another

level he really likes it, and he feels guilty that he likes it, so he denies he likes it, if you see my point."

Emma thought about that for a moment and realized Sam was probably right. "Sometimes you amaze me," she marveled.

"And here you thought I was just a gorgeous but brainless babe," Sam joked. "You want to go in and order some food? I'm starved."

"No, I told Katie she'd find me here after her story-telling hour," Emma said. She put on her dark sunglasses and settled down on the chaise.

"You know, Kurt's cousin is really cute," Sam said, watching Freddie in the pool with the twins.

"You think every guy that walks is cute," Emma replied.

"Not true, not true," Sam disagreed. "I am so discriminating, you wouldn't believe all the guy-types I've eliminated. Anyway, my mind is on a certain southern cutie who will be at the party tonight."

"Just don't push him too hard, Sam," Emma suggested.

"Moi?" Sam asked innocently. "I am not the pushy type. I am the sought-after type. I just plan to look so unbelievably hot he remembers what he's missing." She pulled a tube of sunscreen out of her bag. "Or maybe if I flirt with Freddie that will make Pres jealous and—"

"Sam!" Emma warned. "That's exactly the kind of stuff that got you into trouble with Pres in the first place!"

Sam sighed. "I suppose." She turned to Emma. "Does it bother you to think about not even being able to flirt anymore?"

"Married people flirt," Emma said uncomfortably.

"Yeah, but it's really lame," Sam said.

"That's true," Emma admitted.

"I mean, your whole life, from now on, you're only going to feel one pair of lips kissing yours," Sam continued, "and your whole life you're only going to know what it feels like to do it with one guy."

"It's romantic," Emma said firmly.

"Uh-huh," Sam said, clearly not convinced. She settled back down and closed her eyes to the hot sun. "Well, if you ask me, it sounds kind of like dying before your time."

"Oh, thanks so much," Emma said with a laugh.

"Hey, just because I feel that way doesn't mean you feel that way," Sam said without opening her eyes. "Obviously you don't feel that way, or you wouldn't be getting hitched."

"Right," Emma agreed, even though somewhere inside of her there was a place that wasn't quite convinced at all.

* * *

That evening, Emma dressed in white cotton pants and a pink linen vest over a sleeveless white T-shirt. As she brushed her hair in the mirror she thought: *I am going to my engagement party. Engagement. That means I'm about to get married.*

"Mrs. Kurt Ackerman," Emma said out loud to her reflection. She made a face. "Uh-uh. I can't handle it. I'm not changing my name. Kurt can just get over it." She put her brush down and reached for her brown mascara, drawing the brush over her blond lashes. Then she put on the tiniest line of eye liner, a hint of pink blush, and rubbed some pink lip stain that Sam insisted was "kissproof" into her lips.

"You look cute," Jeff Hewitt told Emma when she came downstairs. He and Jane were sitting on the couch playing Scrabble.

"Thanks," Emma said, getting her pink jean jacket out of the front hall closet. "Where are the kids?"

"Next door at Stinky Stein's house," Jane replied. "They're having a pool party."

"I knew it was too quiet in here," Emma said with a grin.

"It's temporary," Jane assured her. "It's a great idea, you know, having a coed engagement party instead of a shower for you and a bachelor party for him."

"Oh, I don't know," Jeff said with a twinkle in

his eye, "bachelor parties can be really fun."

"Oh, sure," Jane agreed. "I just love an occasion where men get together, drink to excess, and throw up all over each other."

"Now, that is definitely not Kurt's style," Emma said.

"True," Jane said. "He's a great guy." She put some tiles down on the Scrabble board. "Seven-letter word! Eat your heart out, big guy!"

"Why, you brat!" Jeff exclaimed. "How did you manage a seven-letter word?"

"Face it, I'm smarter than you are, which is why I always beat you at Scrabble," Jane said smugly.

"Oh, really?" Jeff asked. He leaned over and began tickling his wife in the ribs.

"Stop! Stop!" Jane yelled, laughing hysterically. "Not the ribs!"

"Yes, the ribs!" Jeff exulted, tickling her some more. Then he leaned over and kissed his wife sweetly on her lips. "I've decided to show you some mercy."

"Gee, thanks," Jane said. "I don't plan to show you any mercy in this Scrabble game, however!"

Emma felt wistful, watching them. *They've been married forever*, she thought, *and they still really love each other. Just because my parents' marriage was terrible doesn't mean other marriages aren't wonderful. Just because my parents fought all the time doesn't mean Kurt and I will.*

Well, maybe we're fighting a lot now, but that's just the tension of the wedding plans—that will change, and—

"Emma?" Jane asked.

"What?" Emma replied, startled from her train of thought.

"I said the gas is low in the Mercedes, so fill it up on the way to the party, okay?"

"Oh, sure," Emma agreed. "Have fun with your game."

"Have fun at your party!" Jeff said. Then he wrapped his arms around his wife, and the two of them forgot that Emma even existed.

She stopped for gas and then drove to the beach, where a huge crowd had already gathered.

"It's one half of the couple of honor!" Carrie called as Emma walked over to her. She gave Emma a hug. "I'm so excited!"

"Me, too," Emma agreed, trying to sound enthusiastic. "I didn't even know Kurt and I knew this many people!"

"Well, you do," Carrie told her. She began pulling paper goods out of a large bag. "Everyone on the island wanted to come join in the well-wishing."

Emma looked around. Even though it wasn't dark yet, someone had started a huge bonfire which crackled brightly. Groups of people stood around talking, one group had started a Frisbee game, some others were shooting each other with giant water pistols.

It all looks so carefree, Emma thought. *And I should be so happy.* "Is Kurt here yet?"

"He's over there with his cousin," Carrie said, cocking her head toward the barbeque pit.

"Thanks," Emma said, and went to find Kurt.

"Hi, gorgeous," Kurt said when he saw her. He put his arms around her and kissed her gently on the lips.

He seems to have forgotten all about our dis-agreement this afternoon, Emma thought, kiss-ing him back. *Well, good. Staying mad would be silly. So why do I still feel mad?*

"My cousin here makes the best burgers you ever ate," Kurt assured Emma.

"It's an old family recipe," Freddy said, pour-ing some Tabasco sauce on the burgers. "I can only pass it on to my firstborn son."

"And since Freddie never plans to get mar-ried, that means he's going to his grave with this recipe!" Kurt laughed.

"Hey, marriage is not my style and will never be my style," Freddie said with a shrug. He flipped some of the burgers on the grill. "My motto has always been: so many girls, so little time."

Emma laughed. "Hey, that's Sam's motto!"

"No kidding?" Freddie asked.

"What's my motto?" Sam asked, overhearing Emma.

"Freddie here believes in spreading his attention amongst the many," Kurt said in a teasing voice. "Kind of like you with guys." He turned to Emma and hugged her close. "Now, me, I've always been a one-woman kind of a guy." He kissed Emma again.

"Hey, Emma!" Howie Lawrence said, coming up to Emma. "Congratulations!" He gave Emma a big hug.

"Thanks," Emma said.

Howie turned to Sam. "Where should I put this? It's from me and Molly."

Emma turned around and saw Molly Mason sitting in a beach chair, talking with Darcy Laken. Molly was a sixteen-year-old girl who lived on the island year-round in a huge, old spooky house on a hill. Though she'd formerly been called Maniac Mason by her friends because she was such a daredevil, she'd been in a car accident and was now a paraplegic, confined to a wheelchair. Darcy was the nineteen-year-old girl who lived with Molly and her family as Molly's companion. Darcy and Molly were also best friends. Their lives were often complicated by the fact that Darcy had ESP and sometimes knew what was going to happen in the future.

Emma caught Molly's eye and waved to her and Darcy.

"You and Molly are an item now?" Sam asked Howie.

Howie grinned and blushed. "I'm working on it," he told Sam.

"There's a table back over there where you can put the presents," Sam told Howie. "Behind where all those kids are standing."

"Thanks," Howie said.

"Emma!" Jay Bailey, the sweet, mild-mannered keyboard player from Flirting with Danger said, coming up to Emma to give her a hug. "You're gonna be a gorgeous bride!"

"Thanks, Jay," Emma said. She looked around. "Are the rest of the guys in the band here yet?"

"I don't know," Jay replied, "I came from a pickup gig at the Sunset Inn, playing piano in the lobby for the hoity-toity set—no offense," he added, apparently remembering at the last second how rich Emma was.

"None taken," Emma said easily.

"Okay, boys and girls, it's chow time!" Freddie called out.

"Put the burgers on the platters and we'll carry them over to the serving table," Sam told Freddie.

"Can I help?" Kurt asked.

"Not a chance, buddy," Freddie told his cousin. "You and Emma just sit around and smooch or something while us peons do the work."

"You heard the guy," Kurt said to Emma. He took her hand. "Let's go sit with everyone over there."

Kurt and Emma walked over to a group of

about twenty people who were sitting around on blankets, talking and laughing.

"Hey, it's the lovebirds!" Patsi, the waitress from the Play Café called out.

"I'm featuring you guys in my next gossip column in the *Breakers*," Kristy Powell said.

"Did you guys decide where to go on your honeymoon?" Jason Levine, Kurt's friend from work asked.

"Europe," Emma said happily.

"And they're taking me along in their luggage—right, you guys?" Sam said, plopping down next to Emma.

"No chance," Kurt told her. "This will be strictly a private affair."

"Pres isn't here yet," Sam said to Emma in a low voice.

"I heard he and Billy were writing today," Emma replied. "I'm sure he'll be here."

"Do I look okay?" Sam asked anxiously.

Emma took in Sam's faded jeans cut sexily below her navel and her hot pink bra top covered by a ragged denim jacket with a dozen different rhinestone pins on it.

"You look great," Emma assured her.

"Sniff," Sam said, putting her wrist under Emma's nose. "It's called 'Vixen.'"

"Nice," Emma replied, even though the cloying, heavy scent was almost unbearable to her. "Where did you get it?"

"I tore it out of *Vogue*," Sam admitted. "Scratch and sniff. I could never afford this stuff."

"Hey, ya'll," a sexy, drawling male voice called. Emma looked up and there was Pres. With him were Billy and Sly.

Emma saw Pres' eyes flicker over Sam and then deliberately look away. "This looks like quite the party," Pres observed.

"Hey, you only get one engagement party, man," Kurt pointed out. He stood up and shook hands with Pres and Billy. "I'm really glad you guys made it."

"Wouldn't miss it for the world, my man," Billy assured him. He looked around, obviously searching for Carrie. "I think I see a gorgeous girl in need of assistance," he said, and took off. Sly took their presents over to the gift table, and Kurt and Pres sat down on one of the blankets.

"So, how'd your writing session go today?" Emma asked Pres, since she knew he and Billy were working on a new song.

"This one is tough," Pres said, scratching the day's growth of beard on his face. "I'm beat, actually."

"Maybe you need a backrub," Sam offered casually.

"Nay, that's okay," Pres said, without actually looking at Sam. He got up from the blanket. "I think I'll go see if Carrie needs any help."

Sam put her face in her hands. "I am completely humiliated," she whispered to Emma from between her fingers.

"Just take it easy," Emma advised, leaning close to Sam so that no one could overhear them. "You are usually the master of cool."

"I know, but I love him! I don't feel cool!" Sam cried.

"Well, just act it, then," Emma advised. "You're good at playing games."

"But you always tell me not to!"

"Oh, Sam, I don't know," Emma said. "I'm not an expert on love."

Sam looked at her. "Em, you're getting married. If you don't know about love, no one does."

For some reason, Emma felt unbearably sad for a moment. But then she turned and looked at Kurt's handsome face. He was in the middle of a fishing story, but he caught her eye and put his arm around her shoulders.

I do love him. I love him so much, Emma told herself. *I'll always be safe with Kurt. And I really believe that no one could ever love me as much as he loves me.*

"I brought you guys some food," Carrie said, handing two plates to Emma and Kurt.

"Thanks!" Kurt said, "I'll have to get engaged more often!"

Sam stared morosely at the sand.

"Sam? Everyone's eating," Emma told her.

"I'm not hungry," Sam said.

"Wow, now I know you're upset," Emma marveled. "I don't think I've ever seen you not hungry."

Sam looked at Emma tearfully. "That's what I've been trying to tell you."

Emma put her hand gently on Sam's knee. "Give it time."

Sam sighed. "It's hard, you know? To finally figure out you love someone after you've lost them?"

A bunch of people came to join them, carrying full plates of food. Pres sat far from Sam, next to Darcy.

"Wow, this burger is excellent," Howie said, his mouth full of food.

"Thanks," Freddie said. "Just think, Kurt and Emma could have gotten me to cater their wedding, but instead they're having all this caviar and pheasant and dishes I can't even pronounce. Now, my idea of a wedding is burgers and brew!"

"No wonder he's never getting married!" Emma exclaimed. "No girl in her right mind would put up with that!"

"How many people are you guys expecting for the wedding?" Patsi asked Emma.

Uh-oh, Emma thought. *I haven't told Kurt about my mother's list. He will have an absolute heart attack.*

"Oh, Kurt and I invited about eighty or ninety people," Emma said evasively.

"Are the Flirts going to play?" Patsi asked.

"Uh, no," Emma said. "The Flirts are going to be guests for once." *Please don't let her ask who the band is*, Emma thought.

"So, which band did you get?" Patsi pressed. "There are a few good wedding bands out of Portland, but you guys are planning this on such short notice."

"I . . . don't know the band, really," Emma said. *Well, that much is true. I don't know who Harry Connick, Jr., sings with.*

"Oh, bad move," Jason said. "you could end up with some super lame band, which could ruin everything."

"I'm telling you, I know all the good bands in this area," Patsi said, polishing off her burger. "What's the name? I'll know if they're any good."

Everyone looked at Emma expectantly.

"I know you and Little Lord Fauntleroy didn't book a band without a name," Kurt said.

Oh, who cares. I'll just tell them. They're all going to know soon enough anyway. And I have a right to have the kind of wedding I want!

"It's Harry Connick, Jr., actually," Emma said.

For a moment everyone was quiet.

"You're kidding," Kurt finally said.

"No," Emma replied.

"You mean Harry Connick, Jr., the really cute guy who sings like Frank Sinatra and is married to some model?" Sam asked.

"Yes," Emma said.

Everyone was quiet again.

I know what they're thinking, Emma thought to herself. *They're thinking about how rich I must be if Harry Connick, Jr., is singing at my wedding. I guess I could lie and say my family knows him or something. But I'm sick of worrying about how everyone feels about my having money! And now they'll act weird, as if I'm not one of them anymore.*

"Wow," Patsi finally said. "I guess you don't need a band from Portland, then."

"Hey, how about if I go get your presents and bring them over here so you two can open them?" Carrie asked, changing the subject.

"Great," Emma said, giving Carrie a grateful smile.

"I'll help you," Billy said, getting up with Carrie.

"Me, too," Darcy added. She and Howie followed Carrie and Billy.

"Yoo-hoo! We're not too late for the big shindig, are we?" an icky, sugary voice drawled from behind Sam.

She turned around, and there was none other than the two people she hated most in this world: Lorell Courtland (who owned the drawl) and Diana De Witt.

"I don't remember putting you two on the guest list," Sam said coldly.

"A terrible oversight on your part, I'm sure," Diana said, making room for herself in the spot near Kurt that Billy had vacated. "I mean, I am in the Flirts, and I know the whole band was invited. And besides, Emma and I have known each other just forever."

"Don't you look cute, Sammi!" Lorell cooed, taking a seat near Sam. "And look at your little top!" She leaned over to check out what there was of Sam's cleavage. "How does that thing keep from just slidin' off, honey?"

"This is my engagement party," Emma said in a low voice. "And I do not want the two of you here."

"You know, she has the worst manners," Lorell chided.

"It's true," Diana said. She snuggled her arm under Kurt's. "The least I can do is offer a send-off to Aquaman!"

Emma fought to keep herself from actually throwing a punch at Diana—something she had never done in her entire life. Diana and Lorell had nicknamed Kurt "Aquaman" the summer before, and they meant it in the nastiest way possible.

To think that Kurt actually slept with that tramp last summer! Emma thought with disgust.

Kurt slipped his arm away from Diana. "This is not cool, Diana," he told her firmly.

"But, Kurt, after we've been so close, how could

you not invite me to your party?"

"We're not close," Kurt pointed out. "You really need to leave."

"But we *were*," Diana said maliciously. "Really, *really* close." She stood up and stretched languorously, showing off her perfectly aerobicized figure in a low-cut emerald-green leotard and a pair of tiny cut-off jeans. She gave Emma a lazy look. "Maybe we should compare notes sometime," she said.

Emma stood up and went over to Diana. "Kurt already asked you to leave, and I'm asking you to leave nicely."

"Well, aren't you the well-bred lady?" Diana scoffed. She stretched again. "Well, maybe I should be offering my condolences. As I recall, he wasn't all that good in bed, anyway."

Then Emma did something that she'd never done in her entire life. She didn't give herself a moment to think about it. She slapped Diana across the face.

"You bitch!" Diana yelled.

Diana made a move for Emma, but Kurt got up quickly and caught her arm. "Just get out of here, Diana," he told her. "You, too, Lorell. I mean it."

Lorell got up and went over to Diana. "Let's go, Di," Lorell said coolly. "No one around here seems to have a sense of humor."

Diana picked up her purse and pushed her

curls out of her eyes. She gave Emma one final look of loathing. "Just remember, Emma, I had him first."

The two girls took off down the beach.

"Bye-bye!" Emma and Sam called after them in high, screechy voices. Diana gave them the finger without turning around.

"You were awesome!" Sam cheered Emma. "I can't believe it! You, the most well-mannered girl on the planet, just slapped Diana De Witt!"

"Em?" Kurt said, reaching for her arm.

She shook him off.

Just remember, Emma, I had him first.

The bile rose in her throat.

"I need to be alone for a few minutes," Emma told Kurt in a low voice.

"But—"

"Just leave me alone!" Emma said. She walked away from Kurt and toward the welcoming sound of the sea.

THIRTEEN

Emma moved the cool cloth from her forehead and looked at the calendar by her bed. Each day until her wedding was marked like a countdown—seven days before wedding, six days before wedding, etc. Her eyes slid over to today's date, which was marked "four days before wedding."

She lay down on her bed and closed her eyes. *It doesn't seem real*, she thought. *I haven't even had enough time to get used to the idea of being engaged!*

There was a knock on her door.

"Come in," Emma called.

"Hi," Jane said, crossing to the chair at Emma's desk. "Is your headache better?"

"I'm fine, really," Emma assured her. She swung her legs off the bed. "Is there anything you'd like me to do?"

"Not a thing," Jane said. She hesitated a moment. "Are things okay with you and Kurt?"

"Oh, fine," Emma assured her with more confidence than she actually felt. "Ever since Diana De Witt crashed my engagement party, he's bent over backwards to be nice to me."

Jane hesitated again. "Everyone gets stressed out planning a wedding."

"One thing I know for certain is I'm only getting married once!" Emma said fervently. "I can't imagine going through all this again!"

"I guess what I'm trying to get around to saying is—" Jane stopped. "This is really awkward. I should probably keep my mouth shut—"

"No, tell me what's on your mind," Emma said.

"I know you love Kurt," Jane said slowly, "and I know he loves you. And I understand why you made the decision to get married now. But . . . just remember, you're allowed to change your mind."

Emma's eyes grew huge. "Change my mind?" she said, completely aghast. "Oh, no, I would never do that!"

"And I'm not suggesting that you do," Jane said quickly. "I just want you to know that you always have the option to—"

"Jane, that would kill Kurt," Emma said with intensity. "It would really, really kill him. I could never hurt Kurt. And everything is already planned—"

"Emma, with all due respect, those aren't good enough reasons to marry someone. The only good reason is because you really, truly want to get married."

"I do!" Emma assured Jane.

"Well, good, then," Jane said, smiling at Emma. "Listen, are you sure about your decision to stay on working for us for the rest of the summer?"

"Absolutely!" Emma responded. "I couldn't stand to be here on the island watching the kids with another au pair. As long as you can hold out until after my honeymoon, and you don't mind if I don't actually live here—"

"I've told you a hundred times, Emma," Jane said kindly, "the kids would be in mourning without their Emma!"

"Thanks, Jane," Emma said. "I can't even tell you how much all your help has meant to me," she began awkwardly.

Jane got up, came over to Emma, and kissed her on the top of her head. "You're one of the family, Emma," she said. "And no matter where you go or what you do, you always will be."

Jane left the room and Emma lay back down on her bed. *I hope I'm half as terrific as she is when I'm her age,* she thought.

The telephone rang and Emma sat up to answer it. Her mother had left a message on the answering machine when she was out with Kurt earlier, saying she was attending a polo tournament in South Hamilton, but that she would telephone Emma at precisely 4:00 P.M. Emma glanced at the clock. Her mother was right on time.

"Hello, Mother," Emma said formally, holding the receiver to her ear.

"Hello, Emma!" Kat gushed in her usual, little-girl, breathy voice. "I must be psychic!"

"Why's that?" Emma asked guardedly, settling back on her bed for the duration of the conversation.

"Just that I send out such strong ESP! You knew it was me before you picked up the phone," Kat continued.

"You told me you would be calling, Mother," Emma said, trying to hide her exasperation.

"Let's call it ESP, shall we?" Kat asked. "So, how are plans for our wedding coming?"

"*My* wedding," Emma reminded her.

"You and Kurt and his parents and Brent and me and, well, everyone!" Kat cried. "That makes it everyone's! Including ours."

"Fine, I suppose."

"You are permitting Lord Owen to do his job? We are paying him a small fortune."

"Yes, Mother."

"Oh, let's just bring him into this, shall we?" Kat asked.

"I don't think that's—"

"Hold on, Emma," Kat ordered her. Emma heard a click as she was put on hold, and then, just a few moments later, the sound of the line going live again.

She's conferenced him in, Emma thought. *Oh, goody.*

"Lord Owen," Kat said, "it's Kat Cresswell and my daughter."

"How charming to hear from you," Lord Owen said. "We're working away."

"Things are going well?" Kat asked.

"Madam, you are talking to us," Lord Owen said in sonorous tones. "Of course things are going well."

"Do you have any questions for Lord Owen, Emma?" Kat asked.

If I had any questions, I'd pick up the phone myself and telephone him, Emma thought to herself.

"No, Mother," Emma responded.

"Then let me tell you about my wedding dress!" Kat exulted. "It's just exquisite—I had it flown in from the new Paris collection—"

"Excuse me, madam, but there is a knock at our door, which is undoubtedly the fellow from the ice sculpture company. We shall have to be surprised about your dress. Cheerio."

"Ice sculpture?" Emma echoed after Lord Owen clicked off the phone.

"Why, yes, I think Lord Owen mentioned something about an ice sculpture as a centerpiece for the cold hors d'oeuvres," Kat replied. "And a floral sculpture for the hot hors d'oeuvres."

"I don't want an ice sculpture!" Emma cried.

"Darling, don't be petulant, it doesn't become you," Kat chided her daughter. "Now, about my dress . . ."

Emma tuned her mother's endless monologue about her dress out.

"They won't be able to tell if I'm your mother or your sister!" Kat finished.

"Goody," Emma said sarcastically, unable to contain herself.

"Oh, Emma," Kat replied, pure hurt dripping from her voice, "why won't you allow me to share in the enjoyment of something for once? Why are you always so nasty to me?"

Emma felt a pang of guilt. "I'm sorry, I guess I'm just . . . stressed out."

"Trudy Rockefeller tells me that high colonics do wonders for stress," Kat suggested.

Emma closed her eyes wearily. "I don't need a high colonic, Mother."

"Well, try and get some rest," Kat advised. "Remember, even a face lift can only do so much for lines of exhaustion!"

"I'll sure keep that in mind, Mother," Emma said sarcastically.

It went right over Kat's self-involved head. "Good! I'm so glad we had this little chat! Your father and I will see you the day after tomorrow, darling!"

"Argh!" Emma yelled out loud with frustration after she'd hung up. "In the words of Sam, my mother is some piece of work!"

I just want to hide, Emma thought, and she impetuously threw herself on her bed and pulled the quilt over her head. An article about marriage she'd recently read in a magazine popped into her mind. The article was telling the bride and groom how to judge what kind of person their mate would turn out to be.

"If you want to see what your bride will be like," the article had said, to prospective grooms reading it, "take a good close look at their mother."

Emma winced at the memory. And then she laughed from under the tent of her quilt. It was too ridiculous.

History does not have to repeat itself, she told herself firmly. *I am absolutely nothing like my mother.*

And then another voice spoke to her. *No,* it said, *history doesn't have to repeat itself—but it often does.*

"I promise you," Carrie said solemnly to Emma and Sam, as they walked in the evening darkness to the ticket window of the Sunset Cinema, "you will love this movie."

"But it was made in the 1970s!" Sam protested.

"That's before Sam thinks she was born," Emma joshed.

"It is," Sam said, realigning the black, peace-symbol-covered baseball cap she was wearing. "Part of it, anyway."

"This movie, *Annie Hall*, won all the Oscars for 1978. It's hilarious," Carrie maintained.

"We'll see," Sam said skeptically, taking out money to buy her ticket.

This is about the only older film by Woody Allen that I've never seen, Emma thought to herself. *I'm looking forward to it.*

As Carrie had promised, the movie was completely hilarious. In it, Woody Allen played a neurotic New Yorker, a Jewish stand-up comic, who fell in love with Annie Hall, who was played by Diane Keaton, a Waspy young woman from the Midwest who'd never been to college. Finally, their relationship fell apart—not because of the difference in their backgrounds, necessarily, but because Annie Hall thought Woody Allen's character was just too controlling.

Sam and Carrie chortled with glee as they left the theater, but Emma was uncharacteristically pensive.

"I loved it," Sam pronounced, as they walked toward the cars they'd brought—Emma had come by herself, and Sam and Carrie had arrived together in the Templetons' Mercedes. "Especially the part where Woody Allen chased after the lobsters on the floor with a broom!"

"What'd you think, Emma?" Carrie asked. "You're too quiet."

"Oh, I loved it," Emma assured her. "Really. I think it's one of the best movies I ever saw."

"I agree," Carrie said.

"Adam would have loved it," Emma mumbled.

"What?" Carrie asked. "I didn't hear you."

Emma steeled herself to repeat what she'd just said. "I said, Adam would have loved it," she said, less tremulously.

"Whoa, girlfriend," Sam cautioned her, "I don't think it's a very good idea to be thinking about—"

"I just meant that Adam loves film," Emma said. "I mean, we talked a lot about movies when we were together. . . ."

"Uh-huh," Sam said, watching Emma carefully.

Emma stopped walking and faced Sam. "Don't look at me like that! Just because I'm getting married doesn't mean that I can't have friends. Or that I have to forget about everything that ever happened before I got married!"

Sam gave Emma a look. "I don't think you and Adam are ever going to be just 'friends,' Em."

"Well, that's stupid," Emma said stubbornly. "What if I want to have him as a friend?"

"Would you want Kurt to stay friends with an old girlfriend?" Carrie asked reasonably.

"Especially one he still lusted after?" Sam added.

Emma's face fell. "You're right. You're both right." She pushed some hair behind one ear. "Listen, you two will understand, won't you, if I don't go out with you now to the Play Café?"

"Sure, Emma," Sam said quickly.

"Of course," Carrie added.

"Because I think I need to go . . . somewhere. For a drive. Or . . . something."

"You don't have to explain to us," Carrie reassured her.

"You're not having second thoughts, are you?" Sam asked her anxiously.

Emma managed a smile. "Nope," she said, "my mind is made up. Don't gain any weight for those dresses!"

"Yeah, like I ever gain any weight," Sam replied.

Carrie looked at Emma with concern. "Are you sure you're okay?"

"Oh, I'm fine," Emma said confidently. "You guys will see what it's like right before your own weddings. It's just . . . it's a really weird time."

Emma hopped into Jane's BMW and drove off. She headed for the beach, parked, and looked out at the ocean. *Why does everyone keep asking me if I'm having second thoughts just because I'm nervous?* Emma wondered. *It's not very supportive.*

As she looked out at the dark ocean, she thought again about the brilliant movie she'd just seen. *Just the kind of movie that Adam would love*, Emma thought. *God, we spent all night talking about the future of American theater and art! Kurt doesn't know anything about this kind of thing—his idea of a good time is fishing on the Moose River! And he's so controlling, sort of like Woody Allen in the movie. He wants to do everything his way and wants me to do it his way, and when I don't do it his way, he pouts.*

Stop it! Emma told herself. *You've just got jitters. That's all. Pre-wedding jitters.*

But as Emma got back to the Hewitts', went upstairs, and prepared for bed, she kept seeing the movie of *Annie Hall* over and over again in her head, and the ending was always the same—Woody Allen and Diane Keaton splitting up.

Emma snapped awake in a cold sweat and looked at the clock. 3:21 A.M. She sank back down to her bed and took a deep breath. Another. One more. Slowly, she felt her racing heart start to settle down to a normal rhythm.

What a nightmare, she thought. *What a terrible, terrible, nightmare.*

Emma lay in bed, replaying her dream in her head, wondering what it could mean.

Actually, what it means is obvious, she thought. *It isn't going to take a Freudian psychoanalyst to figure this one out.*

Emma lay in bed, trying to get back to sleep. She tossed and turned—sleep was impossible. Finally, she flicked on the light and reached for her diary—the one her Aunt Liz had given her the summer before when she was first coming to Sunset Island and had no idea what might be in store for her.

Maybe if I write it down, it'll lose some of its power, she reasoned.

She picked up a pen, leaned back on her bed, and started to write.

Here's my dream: I was eight years old. I was dressed like an eight-year-old, too—all frilly clothes, nice party shoes, all the kinds of stuff that Kat used to dress me in.

I was walking alone in a field. There were flowers everywhere. I picked up a daisy and started to play he-loves-you-he-loves-you-not. Just as I came to the last few petals, I heard a big voice—a voice like God's, it seemed.

"WE CAN'T AFFORD IT!" the voice boomed, over and over and over again. I looked up, little-girl scared, but there was no one there. I started to run.

"WE'LL LIVE WITH MY FATHER!" the voice boomed, as I was running, over and

over again. I kept running, and the voice kept booming. There was a forest on the edge of the field, and I was running for it. The faster I ran, the further away the trees were.

Then a shadow came over me from above. I looked up. It was a giant blimp, a balloon like in the Macy's parade on Thanksgiving. But what a balloon! It wasn't Mickey Mouse or Snoopy, but Kurt! It was a balloon of Kurt dressed in swim trunks, swim fins, and scary-looking goggles.

I ran and ran, but the balloon kept coming lower and lower and lower. It was just above my head, and I kept running. Finally, it came down right on top of me. But it wasn't solid—it was the texture of Jell-O.

I fell to the ground. My knees were scraped. The balloon settled on me. I couldn't breathe. I couldn't breathe. I couldn't breathe.

I tried to scream for my mother, but nothing came out.

When Emma finished writing, her hand was shaking so badly that the last lines in her diary looked like they were written by an eight-year-old.

It's jitters, she told herself. All it is is jitters. . . .

FOURTEEN

"Emma! Oh darling, I'm so happy to see you!" Kat Cresswell fairly ran off the ferry from Portland and threw her arms around her daughter.

Emma hugged her mother back. It was Saturday morning, the day before the wedding. She had resolved that she was going to do everything she could not to get into a fight with her mother about anything, and just try to enjoy the last day before everything changed and she was a married woman.

"I'm glad you're here," Emma said sincerely. "Where's Daddy?"

"Oh, just seeing that our things come off the ferry securely—I wouldn't want to lose that gown! Here he comes," Kat cried, waving one bejeweled hand at Emma's father, who was looking around for them.

Emma felt a wave of emotion come over her as she saw her father. Just a few short weeks before, he lay in the intensive care unit of the

199

Maine Medical Center, teetering between life and death, due to a serious heart attack. *And now, here he is—thinner, wiser, but very much alive, arriving with Mother for my wedding.*

"Mother, are you and Daddy . . . ?" Emma asked, overcome with curiosity.

Kat got a mischievous look on her face. "Well, Emma dear, what was I supposed to do, allow the man to be humiliated by bimbos and teenyboppers?"

My parents are a couple again! Emma realized. *It's incredible! Adam was definitely right about one thing: it's all a matter of who you pick to go crazy with. Because the world is absolutely, completely, one-hundred percent nuts. Adam. I have to stop thinking about him, and—*

Brent rushed up to Emma and hugged her, even lifting her slightly off the ground. Emma felt tears in her own eyes as she circled her father's back with her own arms.

"Daddy," she murmured.

"Emma," he said. "I'm so proud of you."

"Aren't you proud of *me*?" Kat pouted prettily to her ex-husband. "I've agreed to walk down the aisle with you!"

"Ha!" Brent barked. "You begged me!"

Kat laughed, and she and her ex-husband kissed.

"I'm . . . in kind of a state of shock, here," Emma admitted.

"Well," Kat sniffed, "your father does have a few redeeming qualities." She winked at Brent wickedly, and Emma knew in that instant that her mother and father had been sleeping together again.

Gross, Emma thought. *On the other hand, that's how I got here.* She decided not to think about it.

"Lord Owen is waiting for us at the Sunset Inn," Emma reported. "He wants to show you the ballroom where the reception will be and asked if you two could join him for lunch."

"Delightful," Kat agreed. "We can go over the final plans."

"Doubtless," Emma agreed, feeling prickles of irritation at being preempted by her mother and Lord Owen yet again. "Let me just go get the car."

"Where's Kurt?" Brent asked.

"Working," Emma replied, honestly.

Kat made a face. "Really Emma," she muttered, "there's no need for him to be driving a cab when his future in-laws arrive."

"He says he wants to earn his own money," Emma said simply.

"He needs to get a firmer grasp on reality," Kat countered dryly.

Emma knew this was a perfect opportunity to get into a fight with her mother, but decided to let the opportunity go. She excused herself, went to get the car, picked up her parents, and drove them to the Sunset Inn.

"So what's the program?" Brent asked his daughter as they pulled into the main entrance.

"At three o'clock we're meeting in the Waterfall Room at the Sunset Inn—that's where the actual ceremony is taking place—for the wedding rehearsal. After that you have a few hours free, and then Kurt's dad is giving a dinner at a local restaurant called Rubie's. A good friend of Kurt's—his adopted aunt—owns it."

"Rubie's—how quaint," her mother echoed faintly as she got out of the car. A bellhop came and took her parents' bags out of the trunk.

"That's it," Emma said as they were standing by the side of the Hewitts' car. "I'll be back for the rehearsal in a few hours."

"After lunch, we thought we'd stop in and say hello to the Popes," Kat said, mentioning friends of theirs on the island. "They told me they sent you a lovely wedding gift."

"They did," Emma agreed, although she had no idea which crystal goblet or bud vase had been sent by the Popes. "You can just get a taxi over to the Popes'," Emma added.

"How do we know that your fiancé won't be the cab driver?" Kat asked, archly, starting to make her way toward the entrance.

"Impossible, Mother," Emma responded, in a

jovial voice. "Kurt works another job in the afternoon."

"What's that?" Kat asked, stopping. "Or is it something I'd rather not want to know?"

Okay, Emma said, *I just cannot resist making something up and doing what Sam would call busting her chops.*

"He cleans septic tanks," Emma invented, as she slid her way back into the front seat. "But he'll be disinfected and on time for the dinner. Promise!"

Everyone milled around the Waterfall Room at the Sunset Inn—so named because it contained an actual sculptured waterfall—and Kurt spied his dad at the door, looking around nervously.

"There's my dad," Kurt told Emma. "Let's introduce him to your parents."

"Great," Emma agreed. *Please, God, don't let my mother act like a snob,* Emma prayed quickly as Kurt got his father and brought him over to Emma's parents.

"Dad, I'd like you to meet Emma's parents, Katerina and Brent Cresswell. Mr. and Mrs. Cresswell, this is my father, Tom Ackerman."

"Great to meet you," Brent Cresswell said, shaking Kurt's father's hand.

Kat quickly looked over Kurt's dad, dressed in khakis, a flannel shirt, and wearing a baseball cap. She put her perfectly manicured hand in his work-roughened one.

"Charmed," she said coolly.

"Attention, attention!" Lord Owen called out, clapping his hands together. "Time for our rehearsal!"

Emma and Kurt sat in the nearest chairs. Kurt lovingly took Emma's hand as Lord Owen went down his checklist.

"I guess you're not wearing that tomorrow, huh?" Kurt asked her, a grin on her face.

She looked down at her white shorts and denim shirt. "Not bridal enough?" she teased him.

"I keep trying to picture how gorgeous you're going to look," Kurt whispered in her ear. "And then I keep picturing the two of us up in the honeymoon suite after it's all over."

"I won't be wearing my bridal gown then," Emma whispered back. "Unless, of course, you want me to. . . ."

"I want your skin, that's all," Kurt told her, nibbling on her ear. "Every inch of your gorgeous, naked skin so I can—"

"Can we have those in the bridal party step forward?" Lord Owen asked, interrupting Kurt's words.

"More later," Kurt promised Emma.

She grinned and nudged him in the ribs.

Sam, Carrie, and Kurt's sisters, Faith and Lindsay, stepped forward, as well as Kurt's cousin Freddie, Billy, Pres, and Kurt's friend from work, Jason Levine.

"You, too, honey!" Jane told Katie, gently pushing her forward.

"I shall read for you from our prepared list the order of things, and who walks with whom," Lord Owen explained. "Then we will practice. First we have Jason with Lindsay, then Faith with Freddie, followed by Sam with Pres, and then Carrie with Billy." Lord Owen looked up from his list. "Could we have that pairing, please, before we go forward?"

People moved around to stand near their correct partner. Sam moved over next to Pres. And Pres actually smiled at her.

"Now, then, moving on," Lord Owen continued. "We have our flower girl, Katie—"

"That's me!" Katie piped up. Everyone chuckled. "Do I have a partner?"

"Young lady, you are so special that you must must have a solo turn," Lord Owen told her solemnly.

"Wow," Katie breathed.

Emma smiled. It was the first time Lord Owen had said something that she actually liked.

"Then we have Mr. Ackerman escorting his son, Kurt—our groom," Lord Owen intoned. "Followed, of course, by Miss Cresswell escorted by her parents. Now, everyone has our order committed to memory?"

Heads nodded around the room.

"Splendid," Lord Owen said. "Now, we shall go over the proper walk for the bridal party as you come down the aisle." Lord Owen fiddled with a small, portable tape player, pressed the "on" button, and the sounds of a string quartet filled the room.

"Do stand behind me, bridal party," he requested, "so that you can see the pattern. We are not Fred Astaire."

The group scrambled around so that they were standing behind him, watching his feet.

"Very well, we lead with the right, touch left, lead left, touch right, and so on." Lord Owen demonstrated the walk. "Now, shall we try it together? Partners, remember the woman holds the arm of the gentleman, like so." Lord Owen took Jane's arm in demonstration. "Now, holding arms, on the count of four, we begin. One, two, three, four—"

Everyone practiced the walk. Most of them mastered it right away. Katie had some problems, as did Freddie and Faith.

"I messed up," Katie whispered to Lord Owen.

"Quite all right, Miss Katie," Lord Owen said. "The flower girl is allowed a certain uniqueness. For the rest of you, we will try once again, and you will do remedial work at home before tomorrow, won't you?"

They went over the step one more time, then

Lord Owen had them get in place at the back of the room so they could run through the whole processional.

When Sam and Pres came down the aisle together, Emma saw them smiling at each other. Sam held Pres' bicep tightly and looked supremely happy. *I hope they get back together,* Emma thought, watching them.

Soon it was time for Kurt to walk down the aisle with his dad, and then Emma walked down with her parents. She smiled at her mother, then at her father. *I'm so glad they're together again,* she thought happily. *I never, ever thought I'd see this day. Which only proves that people can change!*

"Mother, where's Aunt Liz?" Emma asked as they practiced their walk down the aisle.

"Her plane was due in just about now," Kat explained. "I'll bring her to your little dinner tonight."

Then Emma was standing next to Kurt, and Lord Owen was explaining how the ceremony would work. Kurt kept grinning at Emma, and Emma smiled back.

" . . . and then the judge will say 'you may kiss the bride,'" Lord Owen continued, "which we trust you will do."

"And you'll be Mrs. Kurt Ackerman," Kurt whispered to Emma, taking her in his arms.

"I'll be Emma Cresswell, your wife," Emma corrected him, kissing him sweetly.

"Well, this went grandly," Lord Owen told everyone. "We request that you arrive two hours before the ceremony tomorrow afternoon for photographs. And remember, ladies, hair up, clear nail polish or French manicures only!"

"Gee, and I was planning on green polish," Sam sarcastically moaned to Emma.

"We heard that," Lord Owen said as he sailed by Sam. "Just keep in mind that we are doing the best we can with our limited resources." He slipped on his sunglasses, then peered over the top of them at Sam. "And do tone down the lipstick. Red is so gauche on a redhead."

Sam put her hands on her hips. "Who died and made you fashion king?" she asked him.

He gave her a supercilious look. "Dear girl, we are not amused," he replied, striding away.

That evening, Emma was sitting with Carrie and Sam at a crowded table in Rubie's restaurant. Kurt was in the kitchen with Rubie, and Kurt's family was busy chattering with one another on the other side of the table. Emma smiled at her two best friends.

"You guys look great," she told them.

Carrie had on a red crocheted sweater over a jean skirt, and Sam had on her baby T-shirt with a very full, very short black and white polka-dotted skirt. And, of course, she had her red cowboy boots on her feet.

Emma had chosen beige linen pants with a matching beige linen vest—*perfect for a casual dinner, but not so casual that my mother has a heart attack*, she'd thought as she'd dressed.

Most everyone else at the table had on jeans, including Kurt's dad and his sisters, but Emma figured she'd make an effort to avoid a fight with her mother.

"Thanks," Carrie said. "I am getting so excited about this. Now that everyone is arriving from out of town, it's starting to seem real!"

"I know," Emma agreed. "Although sometimes I still feel as if this is all some book I'm reading or something."

"Well, it's not," Sam pointed out. "It's your life, and a pretty cool one, I might add."

"There are my parents," Emma said when she spotted Kat and Brent at the door of the restaurant.

"Get a load of the parental units!" Sam chortled, watching them enter. "They look like they've just walked into an episode of *The Twilight Zone*."

Oh, no! I forgot to tell them this was an informal dinner at a very informal restaurant, Emma realized.

Kat had on perfect makeup and a perfect gray silk cocktail dress that Emma knew had been made to order for her in Milan. Pearls hung from her ears, and a strand of pearls with a diamond and ruby clasp circled her neck. On her feet were gray pumps in buttery kid leather, and she clutched a gray envelope bag with a real diamond clasp. Brent was wearing a black French-made Ted Lapidus double-breasted suit, custom-tailored, a white shirt with ruby cufflinks, and a maroon silk tie.

"That's their concept of casual?" Carrie whispered to Emma.

"I think I forgot to tell them," Emma whispered back. "Excuse me." Emma got up and went straight to her parents.

"Why didn't you tell us how to dress?" Kat hissed as Emma approached.

"I forgot," Emma said honestly.

"Brent, I told you we should have let Lord Owen plan this dinner," Kat said to Emma's father.

"Kurt's dad is giving it," Brent reminded her easily. "That wouldn't have worked."

"Well, I have never been so humiliated," Kat murmured.

"I'll just take off my tie," he said. "How'll that be?"

"Ducky," Kat replied icily. "What am I supposed to do, take off my dress?" Since she could see everyone at the table looking in their direction, she plastered a smile on her face. "Exactly what kind of place is this?" she asked Emma through her fake smile.

"I told you, Kurt's adopted aunt owns it," Emma said. "They have great seafood."

With the fake smile still plastered to her face, Kat looked around the restaurant. Emma saw it through Kat's eyes—the tacky plastic mermaids mounted on the wall, the fishnets hung in the corner, dusty and tired-looking, the poorly hung photos of locals proudly holding up their catches from the sea.

No, I won't see it with her eyes, Emma told herself firmly. *I love Rubie's. I am not my mother!*

"Come on, Kat," Brent said, taking his ex-wife's arm. "Be a good sport—"

"Is the food safe to eat?" Kat whispered. "Because to me it looks—"

"Hello, Mrs. Cresswell, hello, Brent," Kurt said, coming up to them. He kissed Kat on the cheek and shook Brent's hand.

Emma smiled at Kurt and moved over to his side. She felt ever so much more comfortable being next to Kurt than she did being next to her parents.

"Hi, young man," Brent said warmly.

"I meant to tell you this afternoon how much better you're looking since you were sick," Kurt told Brent.

"He's with me, that's why," Kat spoke up. "And please, I'm going to be your mother-in-law whether I like it or not. So call me Kat."

"Okay, Kat," Kurt responded. He led the way over to the table and held out Kat's chair, then Emma's. When everyone was seated, he picked up a glass from the nearest table, and a soup spoon, and then started banging on the glass with the spoon to get everyone's attention.

It took a while. The restaurant was packed. In addition to Kurt, his father, and his two sisters, his cousin Freddie was there, along with many of his family's friends from the island. Even some of the members of the political group with whom Kurt sometimes worked, COPE, the Citizens of Positive Ethics, had come to the dinner.

Finally, though, the crowd hushed.

"I'd like to propose a toast," Kurt said, "to my bride-to-be and her family!"

Emma leaned over to her mother. "Where's Aunt Liz?"

"Her flight got cancelled—she'll be in later tonight," Kat mouthed.

"Get 'em a drink!" someone in the room shouted.

"Yeah, yeah!" the crowd clamored. "No toast without a drink!"

Kurt's cousin Freddie quickly grabbed two beers off the counter, twisted their tops off, and thrust them into Kat and Brent's hands. Emma looked at her mother, who seemed about as comfortable with a bottle of beer in her hand as she would be holding a poisonous pit viper.

I've never seen my mother with a beer in her hand in her life, Emma thought, laughter bubbling out of her mouth. *Well, there's always a first time*.

Kurt held up a bottle of beer high. "I want to welcome all of you to our pre-wedding party," he began.

"Glad to be here, when do we eat?" one of Kurt's friends from COPE shouted. Everyone laughed, except Kat, who smiled as if she had just tasted bad food.

"Soon, my friends," Kurt continued, "soon. But first, I want to welcome Brent and Kat Cresswell, my future in-laws, to Sunset Island, to Rubie's, and especially to my family! Brent and Kat, great to have you aboard!"

Everyone in Rubie's broke into cheers, and there were shouts of "hear, hear!" from everywhere. Emma took another quick glance at her mother. Kat's lips were pursed as if she were watching a striptease show in a seedy bar.

"Now, let's eat!" Kurt finished. The clatter of plates and the rattling of serving dishes filled with steamed corn, steamed clams, lobsters, broiled chicken, cole slaw, potato salad, three-bean salad, steamed mussels, and homemade bread filled the small restaurant.

"Yum yum! Yum yum! Yum yum!" went a chant that began with some of Kurt's high school friends. Soon the whole room had taken it up, and it didn't quit until Rubie herself came out of the kitchen wearing her huge apron and clasped her hands over her head like a champion prizefighter.

Emma took another quick look at her parents. Her father seemed okay, even bemused, but her mother looked as if she was suffering from the vapors.

"Your parents haven't said one thing to my dad at this party yet," Kurt said in Emma's ear.

"Well, they're not even sitting at the same table," Emma replied.

Just then, they saw Kurt's father push his chair back and walk over to the Cresswells. He was wearing a red flannel shirt, jeans, and work boots, and had a Boston Red Sox baseball cap on his head. He stuck out his hand.

"Just wanted to say welcome to the family," he said, shaking Brent's hand.

Then he stuck his hand out to Kat. She regarded it for a moment, and then reached out and gingerly took his hand. "A pleasure," Kat said.

Those were the only two words that Kat uttered the entire night to any member of Kurt's family.

Emma and Kurt sat together in the empty dining room of Rubie's. It was nearly 11:00, all the people had left, and the busboy—a friend of Kurt's from way back—was still busy clearing tables and mopping the floor.

"What a party!" Emma laughed.

"I barely survived it." Kurt chuckled. "All that food!"

"All that noise!"

"All those babes!" Kurt grinned. "I thought my cousin Freddie was going to get a crick in his neck, he was so busy swinging it back and forth between you, Carrie, and Sam."

"I'm taken," Emma smiled.

"Never stopped Freddie before," Kurt noted, taking one last swig of a beer he'd been drinking.

"Well, I thought it went pretty well, all things considered," Emma summed up, taking off one of her flats and rubbing her foot gingerly.

"All but your parents," Kurt contended. "They looked like they'd rather be eating live cockroaches."

"Just Kat," Emma sighed. "My father was okay."

"Yeah," Kurt agreed, "but your mother couldn't have been more rude."

Emma felt herself start to get a little defensive. "I know she was unfriendly, but you have to understand that she comes from a completely different background from your father."

"That's not an excuse for her to act like a bitch," Kurt replied.

"She was quiet, not bitchy," Emma said.

"Oh, come on, the temperature around her was

sub-zero," Kurt shot back.

"That's not fair and you know it," Emma snapped. "I mean, we've been planning this wedding for two weeks. Did your dad pick up the phone in all this time and call either my father or my mother? It's customary, you know."

"No," Kurt admitted. "First of all, my dad doesn't know what's 'customary' with your set. And second of all, I didn't see either of your parents pick up the phone to call him, either."

"Since my parents were coming to his hometown, it was his responsibility," Emma maintained.

"Well, maybe he didn't want to waste his breath."

"That's not for you to say, Kurt," Emma said, hurt. "I didn't see you picking up the phone, either."

"It's all I can do to stand your mother in person," Kurt responded coldly.

"How dare you!" Emma cried.

"It's the truth," Kurt shrugged. "She thinks I'm the turd of the earth."

"That's not true!" Emma said tearfully, getting more and more upset. "And I am not going to let you treat her like she's a stranger. She's my mother!"

"I'll treat her as well as she treats me and my family," Kurt said firmly. "No better."

"Well, you can start by apologizing to me for

the things you said about her," Emma sniffed.

"I will not," Kurt shot back.

"Yes, you will," Emma countered.

"Sorry, Emma, but I'm not a hypocrite," Kurt answered.

"Ha!" Emma shouted, getting up from the table and grabbing her keys. "Maybe you should look in the mirror before you start telling other people they've got an attitude!"

Emma snatched her pocketbook from the table, pushed her chair away, and stormed out the door.

I am losing my mind, Emma thought, a tear working its way down her face as she drove back to the Hewitts'. *I love Kurt! Why do I keep fighting with him over every little thing?*

By the time she got back to the house, she'd pretty much decided to turn the car around and head over to Kurt's to apologize. *He was as wrong as I was*, Emma realized, *but it doesn't matter who apologizes first. What matters is how much we really love each other.*

Emma ran inside, intending to use the bathroom and then head over to Kurt's (*I'll throw rocks at his window the way he did with me*, Emma thought. *That will be romantic*), but a letter on the table in the front hall stopped her. It was from the Peace Corps.

"How did I miss seeing this?" Emma said out

loud. *"Well, now I'll find out where I'm going. Oh, I hope it's Africa! I hope it's Zaire!"*

She tore open the envelope with shaking fingers and pulled out the letter.

Dear Ms. Cresswell,

Thank you for your interest in the Peace Corps. We have carefully considered your application. Although your essay was excellent and your language skills impressive, it is the feeling of the Corps that you would be better served to continue your college education for at least another year before beginning work with the Peace Corps. We would very much like to encourage you to apply again at that time.

Emma fell into the nearest chair. *I didn't get in*, she realized. *How can that be? How could they have turned me down?*

She heard footsteps on the stairs and looked up to see Jane coming downstairs.

"Hi, you're up late," Jane said. "I drank a ton of coffee and now I can't sleep. How was the dinner? We were sorry to miss it, but you know we'd promised to go to that legal seminar in Portland a year ago. It was very boring, by the way. I'm sure your party was much better, and . . ." Jane stopped chattering and looked closely at Emma. "What's wrong?"

Wordlessly, Emma handed the letter to Jane.

Jane scanned it quickly. "Oh, Emma, I'm so sorry!"

"I just can't believe it!" Emma said. "I was so sure. . . ."

"I know you're really disappointed," Jane commiserated.

Emma turned her sorrowful face to Jane. "But I had connections through you, and . . . and I'm a Cresswell!"

Jane sat down near Emma. "You're not used to not getting what you want, are you?" she asked gently.

"I guess I'm not," Emma admitted.

"They didn't turn you down, you know," Jane pointed out. "They just want you to have another year of college under your belt. I bet they accept you after your sophomore year."

"But that's a lifetime from now!" Emma protested.

"It just seems that way," Jane replied.

"I just can't believe it," Emma kept saying. "Everything's changed now."

"Not everything," Jane reminded her. "You're still getting married tomorrow."

Emma nodded miserably. "Yes, I'm still getting married."

But now there's no reason to get married, she realized. *Kurt and I could wait. I'm not going to Africa. I'm going back to college.*

But I could never, ever call off the wedding now.

Could I?

No. I could never call off the wedding.

FIFTEEN

"Today I am getting married," Emma told her reflection in the mirror. She had on her new silk wedding lingerie—a strapless white corset with fine ribbons and lace running around the edges, and matching tap pants. She put her hand on her stomach, which fluttered with nerves.

But you look like a kid, her image seemed to be telling her. *You are a kid! You can't be getting married!*

"Knock-knock!" Sam said from the doorway.

Emma turned to her, and Sam rushed into her arms.

"Oh, Sam, you look gorgeous!" Emma held her at arm's length and Sam executed a neat pirouette. The pink chiffon dress swirled around her long legs.

"I even splurged and went to the beauty salon this morning," Sam said, touching her French twist. "Notice my hair is up, per His Highness' decree. I even got my nails done—tasteful clear polish, I might add." She held out her hands for inspection.

"You're positively virginal-looking!" Emma teased her.

"Hey, speaking of virginal, this is your very last day on earth as a virgin," Sam reminded her. "You have to promise to tell me every detail when you get home from your honeymoon."

"I will not!" Emma said with a laugh.

"You are such a prude, Emma," Sam chided.

"Here comes the bride," Carrie sang out from the doorway. She ran into the room and hugged Emma. "I am so excited!" she cried.

"Oh, you look beautiful, too!" Emma cried. "I can't believe how great you both look!"

"I even put on mascara and lipstick!" Carrie pointed out, fluttering her lashes. "Now you know this is a big day!"

"Ready for me to do your makeup?" Sam asked Emma.

"Wait, put my robe over your dress so you don't get anything on it," Emma suggested. She handed Sam a white terrycloth robe from her closet.

Sam put on the robe. The chiffon skirt poofed out from underneath it. "Okay, sit," she told Emma. "Carrie, hand me the Kleenex to put around the top of her bra."

"If you're so messy that you get makeup on my bra, I'm in big trouble!" Emma said.

"Better safe than sorry," Sam muttered as she went to work on Emma's face. She put on base with a sponge, then slightly feathered in Emma's eyebrows with a blond eyebrow pencil. Then she used a plum eyeliner and made the finest of lines around Emma's eyes. She touched the lids with pink eye-shadow, then blended more of the plum color into the crease.

"This is more makeup than I've ever worn in my life!" Emma said.

"Well, a white wedding gown pales a person out," Sam said knowledgeably. "Besides, once I've blended the whole thing, it won't look like much at all."

Sam took the mascara wand and carefully rolled it over Emma's lashes.

Carrie sat on the edge of the bed and watched the transformation. "Amazing," she commented. "You know, some girls do this every day!"

Sam took some pink blush and lightly dusted Emma's cheekbones, her forehead, her jaw line and her collarbones.

"You put blush on her collarbones?" Carrie asked, making a face.

"Trust me, I got all of this from *Cosmo*," Sam said. She took loose powder and lightly dabbed it over Emma's face, then dusted it off. Then she stood back to survey her handiwork. "Well?" she asked Carrie.

"Can I look in the mirror?" Emma asked.

Sam made a sweeping gesture with her arm, and Emma stood in front of the mirror. "It looks . . . it looks good!" she said with surprise.

"Hey, I wouldn't ruin your wedding makeup!" Sam said.

"Step into your dress, and then Sam and I will fix your veil and your hair," Carrie said.

"Don't tell Lord Owen that the two of you did my hair," Emma said, getting her bridal gown out of the closet. "He wanted to have some hairdresser from New York flown in, but I told him I'd already engaged experts."

"That's us!" Sam agreed.

Emma pulled the plastic off the Jane's newly cleaned and pressed wedding gown, then she stepped into it and Carrie zipped her up.

"Well?" Emma asked them. "Is it okay?"

Tears came to Sam's eyes. "You look like Cinderella!"

"Don't cry yet, your mascara can't run until at least the ceremony," Carrie said, but there were tears in her eyes, too. "Sit back down, Em, and we'll fix the veil."

First Sam brushed Emma's hair until it shone, then Carrie fixed the crown of the veil on Emma's head. They pinned it securely with bobby pins, then stood back to survey their work.

"Stand up," Sam told Emma.

Carrie and Sam stood across the room. Emma stood up and faced them.

"Oh, Emma," was all Carrie could manage.

Tears fell from Sam's eyes. "You look . . . you're so . . ."

"Stop it, you guys!" Emma told them, tears threatening. "If you cry, then I'll cry!"

"Okay, okay, no crying," Carrie said firmly, willing back her own tears.

Sam sat on the bed. "Everything is changing," she said sadly. "I mean, I'm happy for you, Em, but . . . well, you know."

"Hey, we'll still be best friends when Emma is married," Carrie said firmly. "And besides, you know she's planning to send us to Africa to visit her!"

Emma smiled tremulously. This was just not the moment to tell Sam and Carrie that the Peace Corps had turned her down. She wanted to think about only happy things, like Kurt, like her wedding, like being married.

Married. Oh, God.

"Emma? Are you okay?" Carrie asked. "For a moment there, you looked scared to death!"

"Sure, I'm fine," Emma said.

"Everything going okay?" Jane asked from the doorway. She took in the sight of Emma in her wedding gown. "I've never seen anyone look more beautiful," Jane said sincerely.

Emma ran to her and hugged her. "Jane, thank you so much for letting me use your gown."

"I'm honored," Jane said with a loving smile.

Katie snuck in beside her mother. "Emma!" she cried. "You look just like Barbie did on her wedding!"

Emma laughed. For the past two weeks Katie, and her friends had been playing Wedding-Barbie day in and day out.

"Thank you," Emma said, bending to hug her. "And let me see you!" She held Katie's hands and the little girl came slowly into the room. "You are the most beautiful flower girl ever!"

Katie grinned and blushed.

"Okay, little flower girl," Jane said, "come with me while I finish getting dressed. We'll meet you over at the hotel. Oh, I happened to notice that your limo is already in front, waiting."

"Thanks," Emma said. She turned to Sam and Carrie. "Well, this is it!"

"Want me to spray you with Vixen perfume?" Sam asked. "I splurged and bought some."

"No, thanks," Emma said, reaching for the Chanel No. 5 on her dresser. She sprayed her neck and her wrists, picked up her small white silk purse, and smiled at her friends. "Shall we go to a wedding?"

"Well, I don't know," Sam mused, "there's something really good playing at the mov-ies . . ."

Carrie shrugged and sighed loudly. "What the heck, we're already all dressed up. Might as well . . ."

Carrie and Sam linked arms with Emma, and the three of them headed out the door.

"May I come in?" Aunt Liz asked. She was standing at the doorway to the bridal room at the Sunset Inn, where Emma was nervously waiting.

"Oh, Liz!" Emma cried, and the next minute her aunt was hugging her fiercely.

"I'm so sorry I missed your rehearsal dinner last night," Liz said. "There was terrible weather in Mexico, which is where I was flying in from. We just finished a big environmental summit there, and—oh hell, you don't want to hear about the environment. This is your wedding day!"

Emma opened and closed her fists nervously. "I'm a wreck," she admitted.

"It's fine to be nervous," Liz assured her. "Who wouldn't be?"

"No, it's . . ." Emma looked out the door to make sure no one was listening and then shut it. She sat down and her aunt sat down opposite her. "Aunt Liz, what if I'm doing the wrong thing?" Emma asked intensely.

Liz looked at her. "Is this normal jitters or an honest question?"

"How do I know?" Emma cried. "I've never been in this position before!"

"I see your point," Liz agreed.

"I mean, it all made sense to me before," Emma continued anxiously. "I love Kurt, and he loves

227

me, and I thought I was going to Africa in the fall, only the Peace Corps turned me down, and now the car accident that Kurt was in seems like just some bad nightmare since he's really okay, and—"

"Wait, hold it!" Aunt Liz interrupted. "First of all, take a deep breath."

Emma obediently inhaled and exhaled.

"Do it again," Liz instructed.

Emma did it again.

"Feel better?" Liz asked.

"No," Emma replied.

Liz stared at her. "Look, you can save the details of all this for later. The bottom line is that you should only be getting married today if you really want to be getting married today."

"But . . . but Liz!" Emma sputtered, tears in her eyes. "There are over three hundred people out there! There's a judge! There's Kurt! Lord Owen has a stupid ice sculpture melting in the ballroom! Harry Connick, Jr.—*the* Harry Connick, Jr., flew in this morning on Frank Sinatra's private jet just to sing for my wedding! I've got to go through with it!"

"You don't," Liz said firmly.

"I do!" Emma cried, jumping up. "I'm just . . . I'm just nervous, that's all! Yes, that's what it must be!"

Liz stood up and reached for Emma's arm. "Emma—"

"Or else I've completely lost my mind," Emma said. "That's another possibility, isn't it? Wedding cancelled on account of insanity?"

"Emma—"

"No, no, I'm just acting like an idiot," Emma told herself and Liz. "I love Kurt. I'll love being his wife."

Carrie and Sam rushed into the room and kissed Emma.

"Good luck!" Carrie cried, hugging Emma.

"As we say in show biz, break a leg!" Sam put in, adding her hug to Carrie's. "We gotta go stand where His Highness told us to stand."

"As David Frohman would say, 'It's showtime!'" Carrie exulted. She and Sam hurried from the room.

"Emma, please, think about this," Liz said, a concerned look on her face. "However embarrassing it would be to call off the wedding is nothing compared to finding yourself married to someone you don't want to be married to!"

"But I love Kurt!" Emma protested.

"But do you want to marry him today, right now?" Liz pressed.

"I don't know!" Emma shouted. "I—"

"Well, Emma, it's time for you to go meet your parents at the proper place," Lord Owen said from the doorway. "You look lovely, and we trust that everything will come off without a hitch." He handed Emma her all-white floral bouquet.

"I'm sure it will," Emma managed to say before he left. She turned to her aunt. "I'm fine," she said tonelessly.

"Are you sure?" Liz asked, concern etched across her brow.

"I'm sure," Emma replied.

Liz stared at the niece whom she loved so much. "Em, you can't do this for Kurt or your parents or because it's the right thing to do. Now is not the time to worry about being well-mannered, or to worry about what people will think. Now is the time to do exactly what your heart tells you to do."

For a moment, the room was completely silent.

"I'm sure," Emma finally said again.

Liz kissed her niece and left the room, and Emma slowly walked down the thickly carpeted hallway and joined her parents outside the Waterfall Room.

"You're lovely," her father said, kissing her cheek.

"Truly lovely," her mother agreed, squeezing her hand so as not to muss her perfect lipstick.

As if in a dream, Emma heard the string quartet play, and then the processional began. Couple by couple, they walked down the red-carpeted aisle, right-touch-left, left-touch-right. Then it was Katie's turn, and Emma could hear the huge crowd ooh and ah at the darling little girl as she strew the path with pink rose petals from her basket. Then it was Kurt, proudly walking down the aisle with his father, both of them looking handsome in black tuxedos. And finally the music changed, which was Emma and her parents' cue. All eyes were on her as she slowly made her way down the aisle.

There are Jane, Jeff, Ethan, and Wills, Emma noted, *and Patsi from the Play Café, and the other guys from the band. God, there are a zillion people here I don't even recognize—they must all be friends of my parents. Oh, there's Molly and Darcy, sitting with Howie Lawrence. And Mr. Jacobs and the twins, and Graham Perry with Claudia, Ian, and Chloe. So many people, all here to see me get married. Married. Married. Right now. Oh, God, right this very minute . . .*

Judge Easton smiled at Kurt and Emma. Kurt took Emma's hand.

"Dearly beloved, we are gathered here to witness the wedding of Kurt Ackerman and Emma Alexandra Cresswell," he began.

This is really happening, Emma thought, her heart beating so hard in her chest she thought everyone must be able to hear it. *I wish I were somewhere else! I wish I was just playing dress-up! I'm too young to get married! I'm not ready! Help!*

The judge got to the part of the ceremony that Kurt and Emma had written together.

"When two hearts love, their joys are more

231

than doubled and their sorrows are more than halved. . . ."

Is that us? Is that really *us?* Emma wondered frantically.

As the judge droned on, Kurt squeezed Emma's hand and gave her the most tender smile. She managed to smile back.

I love him! I really love him! So why do I feel like I'm suffocating?

Just at that moment, something caught Emma's eye through the glass wall that led into a floral garden. Someone was standing there. He moved.

He looked right at Emma.

And she gasped: it was Adam Briarly.

Kurt turned to her. "Are you okay?" he whispered.

She tried to nod, her eyes flickering back to Kurt. She looked back at the window. *Maybe I've really, truly lost my mind. No one is there.*

But he was there. Adam was standing at the glass wall, and slowly he lifted up a hand-lettered sign.

"JUST SAY NO" it read.

This isn't happening, Emma thought wildly. *This just cannot be happening!*

"Do you, Emma Alexandra Cresswell, take Kurt Ackerman to be your lawfully wedded husband, to have and to hold, in sickness and in health, in good times and bad, to go forward together as life partners as long as you both shall live?"

And expectant hush filled the air.

A beat of silence, then another.

JUST SAY NO.

Kurt turned to look at Emma.

She turned back at him.

"No," she whispered.

A buzz of hushed exclamations immediately filled the air.

"Emma?" Kurt said, a look of terrible, bewildered hurt on his face.

"No," she repeated. "I'm so sorry."

Then she thrust her flowers blindly at Carrie, picked up the train of her dress, and ran out of her own wedding.

SIXTEEN

Emma ran into Adam's arms. Then she stepped back and slapped him hard across the face. "What are you doing here?" she screamed.

"Bringing a message," he said, not even rubbing his face. There were tears in his eyes. "You actually walked out."

She could hear noise behind her. People were coming out of the Waterfall Room; they would be here any minute. A panicked look crossed her face.

"Come on," Adam said. He grabbed her hand and together they ran to a convertible, which was parked nearby in a no-parking zone.

As people swarmed out of the hotel, they pointed at Emma and Adam in the car, and Adam took off with a screech of his tires. Emma pulled off her veil and put it down by her feet. She closed her eyes.

"Where to?" Adam asked.

"Just away," Emma said.

They drove to the ferry and boarded the first one that showed up. Once they got to Portland, Adam drove for another two hours before pulling over at a country inn in the middle of nowhere.

He turned off the ignition and looked at Emma. Her hair was a mess from the wind, the eye makeup Sam had so expertly applied was smudged around her eyes. Adam looked at her like he'd never seen anyone more beautiful in his entire life.

"I love you," he said quietly.

Emma said nothing. Together they went into the lobby of the inn and Adam registered them. The clerk made clucking sounds about the lovely newlyweds, but Emma was silent. Finally the paperwork was done, and they were escorted to their room.

Emma sat on the bed. She felt like a zombie.

"What now?" Adam asked her.

"I have to call . . . somebody," Emma said vaguely.

"I can't believe you did it," Adam said, his eyes shining. "I got on that plane from San Francisco— I just had to—but I hardly dared hope that you'd really change your mind. . . ."

Emma finally looked at him. "I didn't do it for you. I did it for me."

"I know that," Adam replied.

"I don't love you," Emma said in the same dead voice. "I don't know you well enough to love you. I'm just not ready to get married. Not to anyone."

"I understand," Adam said. "But now there's a chance for us."

Silent tears fell from Emma's eyes. "I am a horrible person," she choked out. "How could I do this to Kurt?"

"You weren't ready—"

"I love him!" Emma yelled, wiping her cheek with the back of her hand. "It's not a question of not loving him. But . . . I'm not ready to get married, and we fight all the time, and . . . oh, God, I wish I was dead!"

"Emma, you can't beat yourself up for not letting him push you into marriage," Adam said in a low voice.

"But I hate myself!" Emma cried.

"That'll pass," Adam assured her. "You would have done something much worse to him if you'd married him when you didn't want to be married to him."

"I . . . I guess that's right," Emma managed to sniffle out.

Adam went to the bathroom and brought Emma back a box of Kleenex. "Do you want to be alone to call . . . whoever it is you're going to call?"

Emma nodded and blew her nose. "Thank you," she whispered.

"I'll be around if you need me." Adam smiled

at her and walked out, closing the door behind him.

She took a deep breath and blew her nose again. Then she picked up the phone and did the hardest thing she'd ever had to do in her life. She dialed Kurt's number.

"Your back is getting kind of red," Sam told Emma, leaning over to inspect her skin. "You want more sun block?"

Emma, Sam, and Carrie were sunbathing together on the beach.

Emma turned over and closed her eyes. Even though it was a week after she'd run out of her own wedding, she still felt as exhausted as she'd felt at the inn that night with Adam.

All of it came rushing back to her: calling Kurt, hearing him screaming, and then sobbing over the phone. She had thought her heart would break. He hated her now—well, who could blame him?

Maybe he'll forgive me in time, Emma thought sadly. *But then again, maybe not.*

After calling Kurt, she had called her parents at the hotel. To her great surprise, they were almost supportive of her. Evidently, Aunt Liz had told them about her conversation with Emma, how she'd been torn apart by second thoughts. And the money they'd spent on the wedding would never be missed. From Kat's point of view, it was simply rather embarrassing to have her daughter run out like that. On the other hand, she was so dead against the marriage that she saw more good come out of the whole fiasco than bad.

Everyone has been wonderful to me, Emma thought. *They treat me like I'm recovering from some terrible illness. I guess other than Kurt, the person who is being hardest on me is me.*

"You want another diet Coke?" Carrie asked Emma, reaching into the cooler.

"Okay," Emma said with a sad sigh.

"Things will keep getting better," Sam told Emma. "You'll see. Everyone is going to forget this ever happened."

"You know that's not true," Emma replied. "People will be telling their grandchildren about the day Emma Cresswell ran out on her own wedding."

"Are you going to say good-bye to Kurt before he leaves tomorrow?" Carrie asked Emma.

"He doesn't want to see me," Emma said.

She remembered what he had told her—he was taking a trip to visit Freddie in Ann Arbor, and he hoped that Judge Easton and a senator he played poker with would help get him into the Air Force Academy in Colorado Springs. He told Emma he never wanted to see her again, that the island wasn't big enough for both of them.

"I should leave, then," she'd told him. "Sunset Island is your home."

"Don't you understand?" Kurt had said in a strangled voice. "Every day I spend here is torture now. People are snickering behind my back. Everywhere I look I see your face. I've got to get away!"

Emma closed her eyes and a tear ran down one cheek. *I did that to him*, she thought. *It's my fault.*

Carrie handed Emma the cold soda. "You did the right thing, you know," she said gently.

"Did I?" Emma asked, popping open her soda.

"You weren't ready," Carrie said simply. "You thought you were, but you weren't."

"I just . . . I feel so guilty," Emma said in a low voice.

"What were you supposed to do, marry him and make both of you miserable so you wouldn't feel guilty?" Sam asked.

"I guess not," Emma said. "But what I should have done is realized I wasn't ready sooner, instead of humiliating Kurt at the altar!"

"You didn't do it on purpose," Sam pointed out.

"I know," Emma agreed reluctantly.

"Right," Carrie said.

"So, Adam wants to come back next week to visit," Sam said.

Emma shot her a look.

"Well, he called me today and told me he asked you if he could," Sam said with a shrug.

"I said no," Emma informed Sam. "It's too soon. I . . . I can't be with anybody now."

"But in the future?" Sam asked.

"I just don't know," Emma said honestly. She sat up and ran her fingers through the sand. "I thought I really understood about love, but I don't. I don't know what it feels like to really know with all your heart and soul that you want to spend the rest of your life with someone, without any doubts."

"Me, neither," Sam added.

"Me, neither," Carrie echoed.

"Well, we don't have to rush into that stuff," Sam said. "It's okay not to know."

If I could only go back in time to last summer when he and I fell in love and everything was so perfect, Emma thought.

"I guess," Emma said. "But I can never forgive myself for hurting Kurt the way I did. I just keep seeing his face when I said no. . . ."

"It's okay, Em," Carrie said softly.

"I wish I could take away his hurt—"

"But you can't," Carrie said. "You have to let him go."

"I know," Emma said softly, tears coursing down her cheeks. She looked up at the blue sky, at the gulls making lazy circles, and then at the ocean, so vast, so unchanged by the concerns of mere humans.

"I did the right thing, Kurt," she whispered

to the sea. "I followed my heart. But I'm sorry, Kurt. Wherever you are, I'm so sorry I hurt you."

She could only hope that someday Kurt would understand.

SUNSET ISLAND MAILBOX

Dear Cherie,
I have to admit I'm a little embarrassed to be writing because I am twenty-eight years old, but I love your books. I'd like to see you put more emphasis on Sam's search for her birth father and have her find out more about the whole Holocaust experience. I was able to relate because both my parents and grandparents were in Europe during the Nazi occupation. My grandmother survived Auschwitz.

Keep up the good work, Cherie. I love your books and I'm not ever going to stop reading them.

> *Yours truly,*
> *Simone Gunzburg*
> *New York, New York*

Dear Simone,
You'd be surprised by how much mail I get from young women in their twenties and thirties—you are definitely not alone! My sister-in-law Jamie (Hi, Jamie! I won't say how old you are!) reads all the Sunset books on the beach. As for your suggestion about Sam, it's a great one.

Watch for an upcoming book where Sam finds out all kinds of secrets about her past as well as her birth father.

Best,
Cherie

Dear Cherie,
I love your books. I can really relate to the problems that Carrie, Emma and Sam have. One thing I would really like to see is to have someone steal one of Diana's boyfriends! My friend Sara Williams and I read all of your books and always talk about them. What would make us really happy would be if you would have one of us steal Diana's boyfriends! Do you have anything in common with any of the girls? Even Diana? No offense!

One of your biggest fans,
Summer Renee Cocks
Elk Grove, California

Dear Summer,
How about if one of you steals one of Diana's boyfriends, and one of you steals one of Lorell's boyfriends? They deserve it, don't they? I really hope I don't have anything in common with Diana! I do wear red cowboy boots, like Sam. And I really, really care about friendship, which is like Sam, Carrie, and Emma, right?

Best,
Cherie

Dear Cherie,

I am fourteen years old, and I wanted to tell you that your books are the absolute best books I've ever read, and believe me, I've read several hundred. Right now I'm on my third bout with your books. Could you write any faster? Also, I can't find Sunset After Dark *anywhere. Everywhere I look they are sold out!*
Sincerely,

> *Amanda Hedleston*
> *Culpeper, Virginia*

Dear Amanda,

My publisher probably wishes I would write books faster, too! I do have tons of great ideas for Sunset books. And I always love hearing your input, so keep those story ideas rolling in and I'll try to keep writing them. Any Sunset book that you can't find, you can special order from your local book store. Or you can use the order form in the back of a Sunset book. Let me know if you have any problem with it.

> Best,
> Cherie

Dear Readers,

Well, I just got back from Hollywood, where I went to all these meetings about turning SUNSET ISLAND into a movie! Hey, that's what your letters tell me you guys want, so I'm trying! I'll keep you posted on all of the developments. Wouldn't that be awesome? So . . . write and tell me who should star in what roles . . . I'm counting on you!

Anyway, Hollywood is quite the experience. All the girls seemed to be really thin, really blond and perfectly toned. We are talking serious muscles. But hey, maybe I was just feeling insecure. Well, we all know that there are more important things in life than comparing bicep bulges, right?

I've gotten some great mail lately. Let me hit a few highlights. Melissa Schneider of Staten Island wrote me a really sensitive letter about how important it is for SUNSET books to deal with real issues, and I agree. Heather Roesler of Green Pond, New Jersey, wrote to say that Sam, Emma and Carrie's adventures help her figure out how to handle things in her own life. And

Kathy Sawyer of Worthington, Ohio, really made me laugh when she suggested that Tom Cruise pose for Kurt. Hey, great idea, but how do we get him??

Thank you, thank you, thank you for all the wonderful letters and the photos. You guys are everything!

See you on the island!

Best—

Cherie Bennett

Cherie Bennett
c/o General Licensing Company
24 West 25th Street
New York, New York 10010

All letters printed become property of the publisher.

See you on the island!
Best—
Cherie Bennett

ABOUT THE AUTHOR

As well as being a much-published, best-selling author of young-adult fiction, Cherie Bennett is an award-winning playwright, an actress, and a singer. She recently completed writing her first feature film for New Line Cinema. Cherie is married to attorney and theatrical producer Jeff Gottesfeld. After living for many years in New York City, they now reside in Nashville, Tennessee.

Join Emma, Carrie, and Samantha in *Sunset Wedding*— as Emma takes a trip down the aisle in a spectacular Sunset Island Special!

It's time Emma Cresswell made her mark on the world —I'm joining the Peace Corps! Kurt has other ideas... he wants us to get married before I go! Is he afraid of losing me? My parents are furious— although my mother will still want a big wedding. Kurt means so much to me — but am I ready?

PQZ228214

13982

0 71831 00399 7

ISBN 0-425-13982-4